TALES OF LAKE TILLERY

MY FRIENDS CALL ME DOT

DONOVAN CORZO

CORZO CREATIONS, LLC

ISBN: 978-1-958297-58-2

Dedicated to the love of my life, Kam.

Many thanks to the Tuesday night crowd for letting me bend your ears.

To Shari, who gave me that pen and told me to go and write that novel. I did, and here it is.

To the staff of "The Book Rack," thanks for letting me hang out for inspiration and research.

To all my family and friends. Thanks for believing in me and for reading the many rough drafts.

To Karl, my friend for over 30 years and my unofficial editor. I appreciate your honesty and experience.

To my Editor, Lila Waterfield, "Thanks for making it POP!"

To the Cover Designer Adeel Ahmad, "Thanks for making them Shine."

Other Titles by the Author

Traveller Role-Playing Game Supplements:

100 Plots E-Book: 978-1-958297-04-9, Paperback: 978-1-958297-05-6

100 Rendezvous E-Book: 978-1-958297-07-0, Paperback: 978-1-958297-08-7

100 Alien Rendezvous (forthcoming)

100 Alien Plots (in the works)

100 Underworld Rendezvous (Almost completed)

Patrol Craft Series

A Time to Shine: E-Book ISBN: 978-1-958297-00-1, Paperback ISBN: 978-1-958297-01-8 Hardcover ISBN: 978-1-958297-02-5, Audiobook ISBN: 978-1-958297-03-2

Shine On: Invasion USA: E-Book ISBN: 978-1-958297-06-3, Paperback: ISBN: 978-1-958297-12-4 Hardcover: ISBN: 978-1-958297-09-4, Audiobook: ISBN: 978-1-958297-13-1

Shining Through: Battles in the Pacific: E-Book: ISBN: 978-1-958297-25-4, Paperback: ISBN: 978-1-958297-26-1 Hardcover: ISBN: 978-1-958297-27-8, Audiobook: ISBN: 978-1-958297-51-3

Up in the Clouds: E-Book: ISBN: 978-1-958297-54-4, Paperback: ISBN: 978-1-958297-55-1 Hardcover: ISBN: 978-1-958297, Audiobook: ISBN: 978-1-958297

Forthcoming Novels

Peace Reigns Through

The Wars End

Table of Contents

Momma's Funeral

“y Mamma always said, ‘Dot, don't be a coarse girl. Be a lady. Only coarse girls swear. Prove to others that you have an excellent vocabulary.’

I have an excellent vocabulary and know how to swear in multiple languages. She always had high hopes for me, but we could be better here in Lake Tillery, NC. The Lake was created in 1928 by the Army Corps of Engineers for Hydropower Generation. The Uwharrie and Yadkin Pee Dee rivers flow into it from all minor tributaries, providing great channel catfish and striped bass.

It's a cloudy February day in 1933 that threatens to rain, and we are all gathered in the Potters Field to bury her. I was in my faded charcoal gunny sack dress, and my ten-year-old brother Anthony was in the black suit loaned to him by the undertaker. It was from a bag of clothing that the local AME Zion Church donated to dress indigent corpses. There's that word again. Indigent. It also means poor. It's a pretty poor life that we have here. But I don't think anyone has been doing well since Herbert Hoover got into office.

Sheriff Funderburk, his wife, and the entire burial staff are in attendance. My momma always had a lot of “friends,” but none of them showed up. Even the preacher failed to show. So, the undertaker had to conduct the service. Momma had a wasting disease that took a beautiful young woman and turned her into a scrawny sack of bones. Her limbs were thin, and she barely weighed

60 pounds. She was so light that they put her into a pine box since she fit, which was all the insurance would pay for. Mrs. Funderburk did her makeup since we had no money for it. She did a remarkable job.

The sheriff and his wife are our godparents, so we will stay with them until May, as I don't turn 18. They don't want Anthony to go into the system. As we leave, Wilfred says, "Dorothy, I think you are grown enough to stay by yourself, but Anthony has to stay with us. We don't want those welfare agents snooping around. So, things must remain on the up and up. If they catch you at home alone, say you returned to get something. "

I spot Delbert hiding behind a tree. I walk over to him. He's my age but a giant at 6'10". We've grown up together, and he's sweet but not very bright. Most people call him 'simple,' which is a nice way of saying retarded. I've never had a problem communicating with him and always understand his words. Most people don't have the patience. I call him, "Delbert, what are you hiding over there? Come out into the light where we can see you."

He shuffles out from behind the willow tree, dressed as best for a funeral. He's got on his Daddy's dark coat, a white shirt, a tie, dark jeans, and tennis shoes. I'm impressed that he cared to get as much right as possible with his sick momma. She generally laid out his things for the next day.

"Why were you hiding over there?" I say as I hold my hand out to him, and he engulfs mine.

I'm not much to look at, being 5'5" with mouse brown hair, a dusting of freckles, and a shape of 15, 15, 15. That's right, a carpenter's dream. 'Flat as a board and never been nailed. '

Momma always hated that joke, saying it was 'Crass.' But here's an interesting fact about me. I can tell a joke over and over and find it funny every time. I've learned that most people aren't that way and can find this trait of mine slightly maddening.

Most people don't have the patience to deal with me because I speak my mind and don't hold back. All the boys at school have been afeard of me since first grade. That's when I met Delbert. My Momma dropped me off at the door on the first day of school. I was wearing a calico dress, and Momma had done my hair in pigtails and put red ribbons at the ends. She had stayed up half the night getting my outfit ready for school. She had dyed my Mary Janes black and polished them until they sparkled. Then she pulled out a pair of bobby socks and store-bought panties with hearts on them. She also provided me with a bonnet. Lord knows where she got the money, but I appreciated the care and thoughtfulness. She wanted my first day to be memorable. Oh, it was, just not the way she thought. That was when I heard a ruckus going on. A rather large boy held onto the pole at the door and did not want to go inside. He was dressed in a suit coat with shorts and sporting a tie that was too wide and large for him. He kept looking back at his momma, pleading with her to let him stay home. She wore the prettiest pink dress, and everything about her was stylish. Delbert's daddy, dressed in an ill-fitting Zoot Suit, was a bit cruel and a mean drunk, so he was shaming him into going in. The principal had had enough and ushered them back to their car, saying they only worsened it. They just needed to leave. He and his staff would take care of Delbert. The poor boy was bawling away and shaking with fear. Once his parents left, he went to pieces. The adults didn't know what to do. But I did. So, I walked over to him and said, "Hey there, I'm Dorothy Jane. My friends call me Dot. What's your name?"

He stopped crying and gave me a hard look, "It's Delbert." Looking for the trap or the prank that was about to be played. His eyes darted back and forth like a wild animal that had been cornered.

"Hey," I said, motioning for him to look at me, "I'm over here," I said as I reached up and pried his hands away from the pole. "C'mon, let's go. Times a wasting. Don't want to be late on our first day!"

Much to the adults' surprise, he let me lead him into the school and our room.

The hall monitor showed us where to hang our coats and then ushered us inside. All the desks had been arranged into a circle, the children had already introduced themselves, and the cliques had been formed. The teacher didn't want to disturb anything, so the teacher escorted us to two desks against the wall. I guess no good deed goes unpunished. I was okay with that. Even if I only had one friend in school, he would do. Delbert had given himself the hiccups and tried calming down so they would stop, but he couldn't control them. I just sat there and smiled up at him. I put my hand on his and said, "It'll be all right. Stick with me, and you'll be just fine." He looked down at me, and all he could see was kindness. He smiled, and magically, the hiccups were gone.

The next thing we knew, the teacher had parted the desks and shooed us into the circle. We had to introduce ourselves. So, I went first, "Hi there. I'm Dorothy Jane. But my friends call me Dot."

"You don't have any friends," said Chester Bastrop, a lanky kid with buck teeth, whose clothing was always two sizes too big because they were hand-me-downs from his brother, and he was too skinny for them. The snickering could be heard.

"Now, class, let her finish.", rebuked the teacher.

"I do so. He's right here, and his name is Delbert.", I said, gesturing to him.

He stood there, looked down at the floor, and mumbled, "I'm Delbert and her friend."

"Well then, you deserve each other, weirdos!" said Tony Bell, the group bully.

Kevin Burrell said, "What's wrong with you, Dot?"

"Nothing.", I replied carefully, as the ringing in my ears started, and the room began to sway. Then I felt Delbert's strong hands steady me, and I knew I would be fine and not have one of my fits.

Charlotte, a cruel red-haired girl, spoke up, "Don't get her too excited, or she might fall out." Falling out was Mountain talk for fainting.

The rest of the children laughed, and Mrs. Wigglesworth clapped her hands loudly. "Time's up, class. Now, let us all rearrange the room into order so we may get on with the day." She had a good soul. She was short, stout, and funny. She jested about her size, saying she was "As wide as I am tall." She had some absolute zingers. Once, she said, "You will never forget my name, children, because I look like my name sounds." She encouraged us to read and question everything. Her class was magical, and she had the patience to boot. She quickly identified who might be a problem and knew how to handle it. If anyone gave a smart-ass comment while she was at the blackboard, they were suddenly knocked upside the head with an eraser. I don't know how she managed it with her back turned and all, but she had eyes in the back of her head.

Our first recess was very memorable. Mrs. Wigglesworth and the teacher's aide got us together to play dodgeball—boys against boys and girls against girls. We were supposed to bounce the ball on the ground and try to make a glancing blow. But of course, the schoolyard bullies had to ruin it. I watched them, and Tony Bell hurled the ball full-on at Delbert, and it popped him in the face. This caught Delbert by surprise, and he was in shock. Being my carefree self, I ran over to Delbert and gave him my handkerchief to help stem the blood flow. As I was doing so, I formed a plan; in one hand, I secreted a rock into my pocket and picked up the ball with the other. I whirled and hurled it with all of my might at Tony. There was a crack and a boing sound as the ball connected with his nose and stopped him mid-laugh. His head snapped back, and he stumbled. His hands go to his face. Blood was everywhere. I snarled, “All right, who’s next?”. The clump of boys looked at me in absolute horror. Tony was mad. He got up and looked at them. “Cowards!” he spat. Then charged at me, saying, “You little bitch!”.

I then hurled the rock at his head, and he dropped to his knees. Falling forward unconscious. I heard the crowd go, “Ewww.”

Mrs. Wigglesworth came rushing up, looked at the scene, and ascertained what happened. She looked at Delbert and saw him wiping his nose with my hankie. She saw the blood, turned to the boys, and thundered, “This is why we have rules. If you don’t follow them, people get hurt.” She looked at Tony's crumpled form and asked, "Dot, was Tony going to try and hurt you?”

“Yes, Ma’am.”

“And what did you do about it?”

“I threw a rock at him.”

“Why a rock?”

“Because I was all out of dodgeballs.”

She did an amazing job of not laughing out loud. But her face said it all. She turned to me and said, “Dot, why don’t you take Delbert to get washed up? It could be broken if his nose has a blue or black line. If that’s the case, take him to the school nurse. Get it?”

“Got it.”

“Good.” She said sweetly. She then turned on the boys with a vengeance. All of y’all will line up outside the Principal’s office to explain your behavior. They looked sullen and mumbled as a group. “Yes, ma’am,” and scurried away.

“C’mon, Delbert,” I said, reaching both hands to tug on him. He got to his feet, and we walked off the schoolyard to the bathrooms. Everyone was looking at us like we were from Mars. Delbert’s nose wasn’t broken, but Tony’s was. I guess rage helps. After the Principal administered the spanking, poor Tony had to endure one from his momma and his uncle Gerhart, who was visiting. Then his daddy woke him up and had a go. That poor boy learned his lesson on day one. Do not mess with Dot or Delbert, or you will regret it.

I wouldn’t admit it, but Delbert was the love of my life, and here he had shown up at Momma’s funeral. It was a grey day. Now that the particulars had been done, old Wilford shooed us into the car and took us down to Lake Tillery Diner. He told us we could have anything we wanted. I ordered a Bacon Lettuce and Tomato Sandwich or BLT with a glass of milk and a slice of apple pie. Delbert had a Tuna Melt and a Coke. Anthony, the Undertakers, and the staff had Hamburger Sandwiches with fries and Iced tea. Sheriff Funderburk and his wife, Clara, had the Chicken and Dumplings. He had coffee, and she had lemonade. The cook and owner, Shelby, had made up some bread pudding and brought it to us. All in all, it was a fair day.

We never ate out. It was a rare treat.

We dropped off Delbert, and Mrs. Funderburk went in to check on his Momma. Delbert’s Daddy had gotten drunk and disappeared one night. They found his truck, slammed into a tree, but no sign of a body. A missing person’s report was filed, and the sheriff did an investigation but turned up nothing of any consequence. Finally, he was declared legally dead. After a while, the insurance company had to issue a ten-thousand-dollar check. They were forceful about it. A lawyer came down from New York City, and Delbert's Momma came to the Sheriff's Department to sign the paperwork and release the check. He acted tough, bullying her into not signing, saying she was committing fraud and could go to prison. Well, old Wilford had enough and tossed him out of the station. Saying, "You had one job to do: deliver the paperwork, get her to sign, and then leave. She does not need your opinion. She has gone through the courts and filed the appropriate paperwork. I've completed the investigation, and he was declared legally dead. What is your problem?"

"Fraud is my problem."

"What makes you think this is fraud?"

"The fact that there is nobody."

"And a judge issuing an order declaring him legally dead is not good enough for you?"

"No. It is not, especially in such a tight-knit community.."

"Mister. You need to take yourself down to the station and get on the next train back to New York City."

"Are you threatening me?"

"Nope. I'm just saying that with that fancy suit and bad manners, you might just get taught a lesson or two."

"By you?"

"Nope, by the local populace. You see, you can't get out of your own way. You are just rude. You think that you are better than all of us. Well, have I got news for you? While none of us went to fancy schools, we do have one thing going for us."

"And what is that?" he said with a sneer.

"Respect for our elders."

“What is that supposed to mean?”

“Your problem is that you hear our accent and dismiss us out of hand. You think that we are just a bunch of provincial yokels. But just because we talk with an accent doesn’t mean we think with one.”

When Clara came back, she had a genuine look of concern on her face. “Wilford, I think you need to fetch the doctor.”

He started to object but saw the look on her face and nodded. “Kids, I will drop you off at the house and get the doc. So, y’all, be on your best behavior. Deal?”

“Sure.”, I said, then seeing his stern look, I changed it to,” Yes, sir.” Anthony followed suit.

He drove the ten minutes it took to get to his place. They had a modest little bungalow tastefully decorated with pine furniture that had been lovingly scrubbed with Oil Soap and then polished to a sheen. There were lace doilies everywhere, and she had several china teapots and place settings. They had a cozy little parlor that was for entertaining guests. So, we hunkered down in there and waited. Since there was not much to do, we played some records, but they only had the gospel, which got old quickly.

So, we went into the kitchen, where they had a nice cast iron stove and a small radio. We turned it on and listened to the weather report, and which shyster threw themselves off a New York City building after losing everyone their money. By six o'clock, Anthony was getting hungry, and so was I. I took it upon myself to open a tin of sardines and a pack of crackers. It was an economical and light dinner. By 9 p.m., Wilford and Clara returned.

“How is Delbert’s Momma?”

He shot me a pleading look, and Mrs. Funderburk took Anthony by the hand to take a bath. Once they were gone, he sat down at the table, saw the remnants of dinner, and very quietly asked in a tired voice, “Dot? Could you rustle up a cup of coffee for me and some hot milk for the missus?”

“Yes, sir, I can,” I said and got to work earning my keep. A few minutes later, he had his cup of coffee with added cream and sugar. I knew the news would be bad because he always drank it black.

“Delbert’s Momma is not doing so well. She might have to be sent off to Troy to the hospital.”

I just nodded and took it all in.

He continued, “I know that you and he are close. But he can’t live on his own without help. So, here’s what I’m thinking. You stay at your place, and Delbert moves into the house in your backyard.”

“You mean Uncle Jimmy’s rum shack?”

“Yes, that one.”

“Okay. But I’ll need to clean it out. Do you have a snow shovel?”

“Yes. Why?”

“Because Uncle Jimmy had a pet goat he slept with, and she left offal all over. So, I need to scrub and fumigate the place.”

“Okay. Then I guess we better get to it tomorrow, being Saturday and all.”

The following day, I awoke from the couch to the smell of scrambled eggs, bacon, grits, pancakes, toast, and coffee. Mrs. Funderburk had woken up at 4 a.m. to get everything ready, and she accepted no help from me. After a while, the whole house was up, and we all held hands and said grace. Then, we dove into the meal, passing the plates around until everyone had enough. Mrs. Funderburk shooed us out of the kitchen and out the door. We grabbed cleaning supplies and the shovel and drove to our small homestead up the rise. Momma's dowery was forty acres. She and Daddy built the place, and then when Uncle Jimmy returned, all damaged in the head from the Great War. They took pity on him and built the shack. He was addled but harmless. That's probably why dealing with Delbert was no big deal for me. This got me thinking of my Uncle Jimmy. I have faint impressions of him. He was my Momma's older brother. While cleaning up, I found his old military trunk under his bed. I opened it up and saw his uniform was in immaculate condition. Wilford saw me looking through it and said, "Dot, you can look at that later. We got work to do." I saw an envelope with an undertaker's seal on it. So, I stood up and placed it in my pocket.

It took all day to clean it out and spruce it up. But it looked respectable by sundown; it would pass if anyone came in to do a State inspection. I sat there admiring it while we drank coffee and finished the last ham as sandwiches.

"So, Dot. Once you graduate in May, what are you going to do?"

"Keep working at the diner."

"What about continuing in school?"

"What for?"

"Well, you are pretty bright."

"That's a nice thought, but school's not my place anymore. I'm done with that."

"What a shame."

"There's no money for it. Most girls go to school to shop for a husband. I don't want that. I got everything I need right here in Montgomery County."

“Well, Dot, you don’t even need to go far. They have an excellent school over at the Village of Misenheimer called Pfeiffer Junior College.

“I know; we went last year when it was called ‘The Mitchell School.’”

“I didn’t know that. Tell me about it.”

“Well, it was a field trip for school, and they wanted to make a day of it. So, we gathered at the train station and rode the rail in. Everyone was excited as it was a day free from schoolwork, and a picnic lunch was promised.”

“Go on.”

“Riding the train was great because we got to see the countryside. Versus if they bused us up there, all we could see was the highway. The trip took about 30 minutes, and then we disembarked on campus. They had a gaggle of brick buildings. Two of them were residence halls; there was a library, a cafeteria, a gym, administration buildings, and a chapel. They were red brick and looked a little artsy.”

“Do tell.”

“They had several current students lead us on tours around the campus. They were called the PALS.”

“PALS?”

“Yep, it stood for Peer Academic Leaders.”

“Sounds corny.”

“I know. But they did it all with straight faces and believed in it.”

“But you weren’t sold on it.”

“No.”

"Well, why not?"

"Because all I need is to take care of Anthony and Delbert, plus help Shelby out in the diner. It doesn't take a college education for that."

"So, tell me the rest."

"Why?"

"Humor me."

"Right, let's see where I was at. Then, they split us up into groups. They took the girls around to see the Humanities and Social Sciences building. They spun the boys off to the rec center so they would look at the Sports Programs. Then, they held a picnic lunch in the quad under the shade trees. They spread out blankets and had a few tables as well. The administrators gave grandiose speeches about how great a school they had, and we were lucky to be living so close to it. They considered it North Carolina's answer to Harvard and had even designed the buildings to emulate it."

"So, then what?"

"Then they brought out the lunch."

"What was served?"

"Why does it matter?"

"Because your childhood is ending, and this is the next big step in your life. What you choose to do and how you choose to do it can affect the rest of your life. Don't be in any hurry to settle."

"Fine. It was a pig picking. They brought out a whole boar, split and laid out on a board, head and all, with an apple in his mouth. The sides were beans, coleslaw, and macaroni salad."

"Any drinks?"

"Yes, they had an assortment of sodas packed in ice in big washtubs lying around."

"So, you could just help yourself?"

"Yep, and I did. I drank three."

"Why did you stop there?"

"Because I was burping too much, making things awkward."

He chuckled at that. "Sounds like you had quite a day, and they went out of their way to make you feel at home, and you didn't seem to care."

"Not true. They were sincere, but I didn't want what they were selling. If Momma hadn't gotten ill, then maybe…"

"Okay. But there is a whole world out there, girl, and I don't want you to miss it."

"How much of that world did you see back in the Great War?"

He got real quiet, "Enough. There was Paris, after all."

"But did you see it and enjoy it? Or rush through on the way elsewhere."

"No. I saw it and tasted some of the local flavors."

I smiled into my cup, knowing he hinted about can-can girls and whoring. Old Wilford never beat around the bush with me. He was always fair and treated me with courtesy. "Don't let the missus hear about that," I said.

He smirked. "Don't worry. I showed her my clean bill of health after I got discharged. No pox, and she told me that if I gave her the gift that keeps on giving, she would send me packing."

"I wouldn't expect any less."

"Okay, girl. I gotta go." He said as he stood up and kissed me on my head.

"Good night," I said, hugging him.

He pressed $5 into my hand, mumbling, "For expenses." then he strode off the porch, into his car, and trundled back towards town. I lit the oil lamp and took it to the bathroom. When I showered off the day's grime and ran the soap over my scrawny body, I ate but could never get any meat on my bones. I looked down in disappointment at my flat chest. Thinking to myself. 'Ain't nobody ever gonna want that.' I used the threadbare towel to dry off and brushed my teeth with a toothbrush that should have been thrown out long ago. I just needed to shave the pig out back and get some glue and 'veyola,' which I think is French for "There it is."

When we were cleaning up, I thought back to Uncle Jimmy. We found plenty of rum bottles, and I also found the envelope with receipts—one from Blackwood Lumber company for 51 board feet of lumber for $4.21. There were three widths of 1-inch planks listed- 12, 14 and 18 inches. There was also an invoice for $3.25 for handles from the local hardware store. It costs $1.25 for a quarter pound of nails. There was also a deposit slip from the Bank of Troy dated August 20, 1919, for $12 with the notation for a burial outfit.

There was a letter from the Clerk of Superior Court where it says Momma appeared and asked to be the administrator for Uncle Jimmy's Estate. A report from the coroner also stated that he died from a stroke. He was only 38 years old. I seem to remember when he died, many men from the town, all veterans, came by. Those skilled in carpentry helped assemble his casket, and a bunch left with shovels to help dig his grave as he would be buried in the Veterans portion of the local cemetery. The community women helped my momma prepare Uncle Jimmy's body for burial. From the time he died, he was never left alone until the burial. We call that sitting up with the dead. It's nice that everyone took care of him. Many men served in the Great War. Most of them served overseas but didn't talk about it much. I'm sure they told stories and reminisced when they gathered at the local VFW, but that was for them, not for us.

Anthony and I now own this little homestead. It's just a two-room house with a pot-bellied stove, a bathroom, and a wraparound porch. Whereas the Sheriff's place was cozy, ours was spartan. All of the furniture was homemade and looked at. I never really cared about it because it was typical. Everyone's house was about the same. I put on my nightgown, stepped into my slippers, and dried my hair. It was cut short for ease; since I was a waitress, I didn't need to have it so long as to get into people's food.

I sat at the kitchen table and thought about many things. Like how many matches that we had on hand. How much oil would we need for the lamps? What about groceries? We didn't have power because it was in her name, and I was too young to get it on my own. So, I would have to make due until May. I was okay with it since I have used oil lamps my entire life, and so has everyone else. Power is just a luxury. But now I realize I would have to do everything independently. Cooking, cleaning, shopping, and making clothes. Being an adult would be hard work, and Anthony was only ten.

Delbert Moves In

The next day, Delbert moved in, and we had to go into town for groceries. I only had $5, which should hold us for a bit. With bacon and coffee both costing 19 cents a pound, bread 9 cents a loaf, eggs were 15 cents a dozen, the hamburger was 11 cents a pound, and sugar was 47 cents for a ten-pound sack, while flour was 63 cents for a 24-pound sack and butter cost 24 cents a pound. But we didn't buy butter or cream. We made it from the milk of our cow. We also had a small garden where we grew our own vegetables. Momma had a fig tree, and several pecan, apple, and peach trees were on our property. All in all, we were pretty set. I didn't need to buy much except for the staple items. We even had a sugar cane crop down by the river and made sorghum and molasses.

Now, I just needed to get home and prepare dinner. Then, go back to work at the diner. Shelby had given me a week off with pay on account of the funeral. But I knew he needed the help, and I would have to work twice as hard. While thinking about things we needed, I thought some chickens would be nice as we could use the eggs and sell the excess. Fifteen cents was 15 cents and, over a year, would add up to almost $8.00, provided the cost of eggs remained constant.

I remember reading about a Crazy Cake recipe that used no eggs, milk, or butter. It had only nine ingredients: flour, cocoa powder, sugar, baking soda, salt, white vinegar, vanilla extract, vegetable oil, and water. I wasn't much of a cook or baker, but I needed to learn, and Anthony needed some cheering up.

So, I set out to make one. It came out all right. Anthony could smell it baking while I cooked the rice and beans with sausage.

"Rice and beans again?" he harumphed.

"Well, now, smarty. I'm not that great a cook. So, I'm learning one dish at a time. Plus, I made you a cake, and I'll let you have a nice big piece if you promise to eat up."

He looked dejectedly down at the bowl but nodded in agreement as he began polishing off his portion when Delbert reached out and stopped his spoon, saying, "No! We have to say grace first."

Anthony looked up at me, and I nodded. So, we all held hands, and I said, "Well, Delbert, since it was your idea, then I think you should lead us in prayer."

"Okay, Dot, I will."

We all bowed our heads and closed our eyes, and Delbert led the prayer, "Dear Father in Heaven, Hallowed be thy name. We come together as a family and stand before you to give thanks for one more day in your presence. I am sorry you saw fit to take Dot's Momma away from us, but I understand she was suffering and might be seen as a mercy. Thanks all the same. We thank thee for the food before us, and may you bless the hands that gathered it, prepared it, and paid for it. Amen!"

"That was thoughtful of you, Delbert. I'm touched. Now, let's dig in before it gets cold."

Dinner was a simple affair, but we did have rich, creamy butter that was better than store-bought and some freshly baked bread that the Clemmons family sent over. They were our neighbors round about the hollow. They grew corn and durum wheat in the summer, squash, cucumbers, peppers, beans, and pumpkins in the fall, and cabbage and cauliflower in winter. Theirs was over 400 acres but still was considered a hobby farm. At the same time, our little homestead was barely considered a sustenance plot, which reminded me that I needed to find out about the taxes on the land and when we needed to pay them. This being an adult is not all it's cracked up to be.

I can smell the cakes are almost ready, and I get up to take them out of the stove. I put it on the sideboard to cool and return to dinner. Delbert has already polished off half of the bread, and I say, "Delbert! Quit eating all of the bread; we've got a cake for dessert. Land sakes save some room."

"Okay! Sorry." He looked down at the table and folded his hands in shame at the rebuke.

"Don't be sorry, just considerate.", I said slightly more sharply than I intended.

I quickly changed my tone and said in a real, sugary, sweet voice, "Delbert. I'll make a deal with you. You can start your meal off with a big glass of milk. Just chug away. Then have dinner. You can then have a second glass of milk with dessert. Then you should be full. Sometimes, you must wait a while for your stomach to catch up with your brain."

"Okay.", he said, grinning at how I said it.

Anthony just looked back and forth and shook his head, mumbling, "Gross."

I stood up and refilled Delbert's glass with milk.

We continued with supper while waiting for the cake to cool off. Then, when the time was right, I grabbed one of the nice big white plates Momma had in the cupboard. It was her pride and joy. She had won it in a radio contest they held in Troy. She had taken us down there one day out of the blue. We got on the bus, and she took us to the movies and dropped us off, saying that she had errands to run. Now that I think about it, she probably went to see the doctor about her medical condition. On the way out, she dropped her ticket into a fishbowl without a second thought. The local radio station was holding a promotion, and the main prize was a table setting for four, and this one came with the holiday extras. A porcelain gravy boat, sugar, and creamer set with a turkey platter. When she returned to retrieve us, the announcement was made, and she looked down at the ticket and was beaming with pride. She was so grateful and proud of her prize. Daddy didn't seem to care at all. Which kind of hurt Momma's feelings.

"It's just a set of plates. They don't have any decorations on them. They're just plain white."

"Well. They are mine, and I won them."

He went back to reading his paper with indifference.

I saw her lovingly washing them and reverently putting them away. Up high. She looked at me and said, "Dot. This dish set is the nicest thing in the house, and we won't use it often, just when we have company or special occasions. Promise me that you won't use them as everyday dishes."

"Okay, Momma, I promise."

I placed the plate under the cake pan and flipped it over. I gently patted the sides and bottom, and we heard it plop out. It looked okay but a little lopsided. Then it started to lean to one side, slowly separating the top half and falling over. The insides were still a little gooey. I picked up a knife and a cake server, cut the cake, and dropped it into mismatched bowls. I handed Anthony and Delbert each a spoon, and we dove into the dessert.

Anthony just stared down at it. I was a little perplexed.

"What's wrong?"

He wrinkles up his face and looks like an old man when he does that. "Nothing."

"Go on. Spit it out."

"Well, it tasted all right. But it looks like a loose poop cake."

Delbert snorted, and some milk ended up coming out of his nose. He choked, grabbed a handkerchief from his pocket, and took care of business.

"You okay there, Delbert?"

He nodded and said, "That was funny, Tony."

Anthony gave Delbert a sidelong glance, then thought better of what he would say and shrugged, "Thanks, Delbert."

Then, we hear the Sheriff's car coming up the drive. I got up and put a pot of coffee on. Within a few minutes, he came up on the porch and let himself in. "Hello, boys, Dot.", he said as he took his hat off.

"Evening.", I said as a greeting, "Can I get you some coffee?"

He sat down at the dinner table tiredly. I poured him a cup and handed it over. He nodded thanks and then stared in bewilderment at the confection experiment gone wrong. He finally worked up the nerve to ask, "What in tarnation is that?"

"Loose poop cake.", snickered Delbert in response.

I put a bowl before him and said sternly, "It tastes way better than it looks."

He shrugged, closed his eyes, and spooned some into his mouth. He then nodded in agreement. He started chuckling. "Damn, Dot. This cake is mighty good. It just won't win any awards for presentation."

I playfully popped his arm with a dish towel.

"I deserved that. And I am grateful…for the experience."

"You are most welcome," I said in a mock, hurt tone, clutching imaginary pearls at my neck.

He lifted his coffee cup in a quest for a refill, which I obliged.

"Anthony, why don't you help Delbert get settled in."

"Why don't you just say, 'Anthony, make yourself scarce; there are grownups that need to talk'?" he said, looking down at the floor and kicking the air.

"That too."

"Come on, Delbert," Anthony said, grabbing his hand and leading him to the shack.

"Okay, Wilford. What's the damage?"

"Well. I was able to get the tax office to roll over the amount until the following year.", he began.

"How much?" I asked.

"Too much.", he said. "But we'll handle it."

"How?"

"Well, we could ask the church to donate…"

But I cut him off, "A donation? Nobody has a pot to piss in, and the reverend is getting his wages covered by the National Assembly."

"I know. Which is why I'm thinking of asking them to help out."

"What for?"

"Dot. We've got to face reality. I've bought us a little time, and we must consider every option. Pride goeth before the fall."

"I'm not too proud to take charity. It is a leg up and not a perpetual handout."

"I know you've got your principles, but we all help each other. In any way we can. Now, Shelby has a jar to 'Help out' at the diners' register since most of those folk are just passing through; maybe they can throw a few shekels our way. The rest of the merchants are collecting as well. It's real hush, hush, and no one is saying anything. They want to do their part. That's all, and you are still a minor. People like you."

"Not quite. They fear and tolerate me as long as I don't make too many waves."

"All in all, not a bad place to be." He said as he rose. He looked down at the recipe cards that were laid out on the kitchen table. "What are you doing?"

"Preparing my arsenal."

He groaned. He then called out, "Anthony. Come on, boy. We've got to go." He said as he reached into his back pocket and handed me the tax invoice and the paperwork for Momma's estate. "Keep these in a very safe place."

"I will.", I told him.

They left with Antony scrambling into the front seat and waving as they drove away.

Now, it was just Delbert and me. And we had to survive for three months; all I had to my name was $3. Any money that I had saved up was now gone. All of it went for the expenses surrounding Momma's illness and subsequent burial. I knew she had a small policy through the Bank of Troy and maybe another institution. But getting checks from people always seemed to be a waiting game.

They were waiting for you to give up, and you were waiting for the money to be delivered so you could survive.

It was back to school on Monday and then to work at the diner afterward. I sat there staring at the recipe cards and the paperwork, remembering we had no money for medicine when Anthony was little. Doc Stevens always had a spare bottle from his dispensary, but Daddy refused to pick it up without paying. He knew it was expensive and had called the pharmacy in New London. He was livid when he found out the actual cost. Doc Stevens was only charging 10% of that to us. When Daddy confronted him, the answer was simple. He was a man of medicine; he used his money to keep the practice going and wrote proposals to get rural healthcare grants from the State and Federal Governments. He even showed Daddy the paperwork to prove it. That's when Daddy and Delbert's father made a pact. They were going to round up some money. Volstead Act or not. They were in cahoots making moonshine. Of course, I didn't find out until much later.

It was Sunday and my last day off, so I decided to do what grownups do and read the paper while drinking coffee. The main story on the front page of the Troy Register was about the Illinois Life of Chicago, whose monumental failure of $150,000,000 was followed by the indictment of several of its officers on charges of conspiracy and embezzlement of funds to support hotel properties of which they had an interest. It went on in detail ad nauseum about the Reconstruction Finance Corporation and Railroad bonds. Boring. So, I turned it over to the Homemaking section. I was looking for recipes. I needed something economical with minimal prep and less than five ingredients. I found one for Peanut Butter and Chili Sandwiches: It instructed you to mix peanut butter and chili sauce to form a paste, then spread it on graham crackers and garnish with lettuce and pickle. I can't believe that they paid someone to write that. A five-year-old has enough sense to put that together.

"Let's see what else there is," I grumble. More of the same. Sardines on Toast and Cheese and Tomato Sandwiches. "Which beauty queen came up with these?" I wondered aloud. Then I saw the name. Ashby Meyers. Yep, that sounds about right. I looked at her byline; lo and behold, she was a contestant in Miss Teen America. Shocking.

I finally found what I was looking for. Brown Betty. It's an apple pudding, but you can use any other fruit or combination. Peaches, apricots, and rhubarb are delicious. It called for apples, melted butter, breadcrumbs, cinnamon, fruit juice or water, sugar, or molasses. Melt the butter and stir in the pint of breadcrumbs. Then, starting with the crumbs on the bottom, add the sliced fruit, sprinkle sugar and cinnamon or other spices, and keep layering until done. Then, pour the ½ cup of fruit juice or water over everything. Cover and bake on low for 30 minutes. Then, pull it out, remove the cover, and bake for 45 minutes more. There was another version of the recipe. But I'll try this one out first.

I get to work in the kitchen since it's raining, and an hour and a half later, the dessert is done and cooling on the sideboard. I heard the milk cow lowing and wondered why. Delbert usually took great care to ensure that she was milked at the appropriate times. So, I go out the back door through the rain to the cabin. I opened the door and saw Delbert mesmerized by Uncle Jimmy's trunk. It looked sweet, and I said, "Delbert, Millie's crying."

He looked up, startled, and I saw what had gotten his attention. It's a black broom-handled Mauser machine pistol that he is lovingly caressing.

The reality is setting in, and my blood runs cold. I carefully and softly whisper, “Delbert, honey, drop that, please. It’s dangerous.”

He looks at me quizzically.

Tears are in my eyes, and he gets up and comes to me, still holding the weapon. He hugs me with one hand. I let him, and with my free hand, I slowly take the gun away from him and place it in my apron pocket.

“What’s wrong?” he asks.

“Nothing. I don’t want you to be playing with something that dangerous.”

“It’s a beautiful machine.”

“I’m sure it is. Look, Delbert, why don’t you go and milk Millie and get me some cream? I made a Brown Betty dessert and need cream to go with it.”

“Okay.”, he said and ambled away.

I lean against the doorpost and let out a great sigh of relief. I pulled on the lever and ejected the magazine; it was full. Then I jack the slide back, catch the bullet in the air, and place it in my pocket. Delbert and I will talk about this weapon, and then I will hide it or give it to Old Wilford. I grab a bucket with frozen water upside down on a post, and the block of ice comes sliding out. Now I have the makings of a plan. I return to the house and get to work making lunch, which is peanut butter and chili sandwiches. I slice some potatoes, dry them off, slide them into a pot of oil, and make chips with the sandwiches.

After a time, Delbert comes in with the fresh milk and lays the pail by the icebox, saying, “We have to wait for the cream to rise.”

“Okay, let’s eat.”

Delbert likes the lunch I prepared. So maybe that twit from the paper wasn't so wrong after all. Delbert got up to separate the cream from the milk, and while his back was turned, I laid the machine pistol on the table. When he turned back around and saw the gun, his eyes gleamed. But I slammed my hand on the table and, in a very stern voice, said, "Delbert, sit down. We have to talk."

He did so, knowing he was about to be in trouble. He looked down and placed his hands on the table. "Delbert, look at me. This here is not a plaything. It is a weapon that has one sole purpose. To kill another man. "

He looked confused. "Delbert. I don't ever want to see you handling this thing again. I mean it."

"But it's pretty."

"It's dangerous."

He didn't seem to be convinced. So, I whirled out from the table, grabbed his arm, and marched out to the field where I set up that block of ice on the post. We stopped about ten feet away. "Delbert, this is a firearm. It makes a very loud noise, and I know you don't like loud noises. But I'm going to show you how dangerous this thing is." I slammed the magazine home, jacked the slide back, and fired at the block. There was a rather loud pop, and it exploded.

Delbert was startled at both the sound and the devastation. I had set it up, and now it was time to beat the lesson home. I said very sternly, "Delbert. This pistol has a lot of power and is the power of destruction. Can you imagine if that was Anthony's head? Or mine?"

He dropped to his knees at the realization and started crying. "I'm sorry."

I consoled him. "Delbert, don't be. You didn't know."

"I don't want to hurt nobody."

"I know, dear. I know."

"You're not mad at me?"

"No, sweetie. I could never stay mad at you. But I need you to promise me you will never pick up a gun again."

"I promise."

"Do you mean it?"

"Yes. Cross my heart and hope to die."

"That's good enough for me. Now let's go inside and have some Brown Betty."

Later, when he wasn't looking, I secreted the pistol in an empty Charles Chips can. I would talk with old Wilford about this, and we could decide what to do with the gun.

Lake Tillery Diner

The diner was at a crossroads directly across the street from the service station. The Bus station was attached to it, with regular bus service to Troy, Spartanburg, and Charlotte, making it a hopping spot. Not to mention that all the goods and services for the region flowed through here. It was nothing special in a typical layout with counter and booth service. There was a soda fountain, plenty of coffee, freshly made cakes, and pies. But with the economic downturn, old Shelby made bread pudding with raisins and rum sauce to keep costs down. Nobody minded or complained. Shelby would turn the radio on and listen to the news or baseball games when it got slow. But this diner was constantly busy., with trucks, cars, and bicycles clogging the roads. The trucks mostly carried timber, and sometimes, there were soldiers in convoys who would stop in and give us a real treat with their spit-shined boots and clean, crisp uniforms. But this place was a waypoint for most goods and services traveling between here, Greensboro, Charlotte, and Raleigh. Furniture was made up in High-Point and shipped on down. Trucks need fuel and water, and the drivers have to eat.

I was sitting there doing my side work of refilling the sugar, salt, and pepper and marrying the ketchup bottles. I hear the radio squawk: Dateline: Moweaqua, Ill., last week an explosion imprisoned 54 coal miners beyond all hope of rescue. Their fellow workers dug frantically for seven grueling days to get to the doomed men, but all they found were lifeless bodies. At the time of writing, the corpses of all but seven men had been brought to the surface. The little town was stricken by the tragedy, which left there 33 widows with a total of 75 children.

“That’s just terrible.”, remarked a dour woman, a customer. Dear, can you turn that thing off?”

“Certainly, ma’am.”, I responded and went to do as she asked. I didn’t mind; it’s not like there was any good news on anyway.

The radio squawked again: NEWS FLASH: President-Elect Franklin Delano Roosevelt was almost assassinated while on vacation. He had stopped at Bayfront Park in Miami to make a speech, and a man stepped forward holding a gun. Shots rang out, and Chicago Mayor Anton Cermark was wounded and later died at the hospital. Four other people are also injured. Here’s an interview with a real-life hero housewife, Lillian Cross. “I stood beside the man and saw him shooting at the president. So, I swatted him with my handbag to get the gun up in the air so he wouldn’t hurt any bystanders.”

I held my hand up. She nodded assent.

“The President appears to be unscathed, and the secret service and local police ushered the gunman way to jail. The crisis has been averted. Now, back to our regularly scheduled program. ‘The Edge of Night.’

That’s when I shut it off for good.

One day around 5 pm, a busload of jocks from Greensboro stopped in all rowdy-like. They were hooting and hollering, either from winning their game or trying to psyche themselves up for one. They were a tough bunch of basketball players. Until one of them got fresh with me. I was bringing out the coach’s meals when I passed by one whom I assumed was a team Captain, and he popped me on the behind. I was startled initially, so I set the plates down quickly and said, "Excuse me, gentlemen. I have to take care of something." I said as I reached into my apron pocket and clenched my fist over the roll of nickels. But I thought better of it. Since he had accosted me, I would do the ladylike thing and respond in kind. Then I whirled around and slapped him so hard that everyone heard his teeth rattle. He stumbled, but I knocked that smirk off of his face.

I retreat behind the counter and grab hold of the metal coffee pot. They could see my huffing and puffing in anger and rage. Well, he stormed towards me, not to be outdone, but was stopped by his teammates. "No way! That's ones crazy." So, as a group, they all decided it was time to retreat. Shelby came out from behind the counter with a baseball bat and blocked access to me. Harriet, a short, stout redhead with great curls, hurried me out the back to check on me. "Where did they get you?"

"Back here," I said as I pulled up my skirt and slid my panties down so she could see the perfect handprint of that fellow.

She said, "Stay here and calm down." Then she marched back into the building and had words with him.

"You need to leave!" she was only 4'11", but people took notice when she raised her voice.

The coaches started to protest. "Not all of y'all. Just him!"

They nodded and told him, "Out! Get back on the bus, and we will deal with this later."

Shelby nodded and went back behind the counter as the boy slinked away.

A few minutes later, he came out to check on me. "Girl, are you all right?"

"No.", I said with tears in my eyes.

This big bear of a man just hugged me and said softly, "Just let it all out." Shelby had served in the Navy during the Great War and had the tattoos to boot. He was about 5' 10" and barrel-chested. He always kept his hair trimmed in a buzz cut and was one of few words. He had a little pot belly from too much beer and alcohol but could outbox any man in the area. He was always talking about his niece in Hong Kong and got letters from them via airmail every so often. His sister was a missionary there, and he was very proud of her.

After a time, I quit crying, looked up at him, and whispered, "Thank you."

He just nodded sheepishly, and we went back to work.

Insurance Snafu

A few weeks passed, and I finally got the checks for Momma's small policy. One was from the Bank of Troy for $25; it was included as a benefit for her being a bank customer. $25, that was all that her life was worth. Well, if that was all it paid, then at least it cost her nothing.

The other was from Life of Virginia Insurance Company for $75. I know she had a little over $2,000 at face value. It seemed pretty meager. Her funeral cost us $250, and that was after the casket was paid for. This wouldn't even make a dent, but I wrote down the deposit slips and considered putting them in the post. Something in the bank was something. But I felt that her policies should have paid more. I would review them and see what sense I could make of them. I remember reading in the paper that life insurance policy loans were through the roof, and people were cashing them in for the value and getting paid pennies on the dollar. If someone had a policy worth $2500, the surrender value would only be $175. So, what happened to the $100? Why was it missing? Maybe a phone call was in order, or quite possibly a trip to Troy to go over it with the local Agent. I sorted her things and saw that I still had the policy. So, I decided to take that bus trip. Because we didn't cash it in, we requested to exercise the rights of the death benefit. I was off of school due to a teacher workday.

The next day, I got up early and wore my best Sunday Dress and hat. While looking myself over in the mirror, I could see that it was a little too short and was starting to look a little worn. Would anyone notice? Well, it was my best; it would just have to do. I walked down to the Bus stop and caught the express to Troy. It was over 25 miles, and I should be there in about 45 minutes. Most people just got on and went to sleep. Many of them were shift workers and needed as much rest as possible. The cost was only a nickel, and that wasn't too bad. Most folks could afford it. I let my mind wander. I was thinking about when that policy was taken out.

Daddy had taken out a policy on himself when he learned I was on the way. He got what was called a Ten year paid in full, or so he thought. Supposedly, you paid the premiums for ten years, and then the policy was fully paid. The problem was that they also had one called Ten-year full pay. This policy had a feature that if you missed any premium payments, it would remain in force by making the payment for you out of the policy's dividends. It would eat up the profits until nothing was left. They should have never been allowed to have two policies named so similar that people could get confused.

He also took out a small policy on me that cost about $5 a year and should be fully convertible once I turned 18. My understanding of what that means is that my cost for insurance could never be raised and will remain in force so long as I continue to pay the premiums.

Now, momma's policy was started when I was ten, and it didn't cost much and wasn't worth a lot, either. But I had to get to the bottom of it. I arrived just as the agent was opening the door. His name was Jaimie Funderburk. He was a rather handsome-looking man in his late twenties. Obviously, of the golf set, and I could tell just by looking at him and the pictures on the wall that he was at least a second-generation insurance man. Good. That was just what I needed. This was the family business. Not some trust fund baby out on a lark trying to impress his fellows. He greeted me with a smile and said," Good morning, miss, welcome to the Agency. I was preparing myself a cup of coffee. Would you like some or maybe tea?"

"Coffee would be fine. Thanks."

I had donned my white lace gloves as I was trying to make a good impression.

"I'm sorry, but I didn't get your name."

"It's Dorothy-Jane."

He came forward with two cups of coffee displayed magnificently on Chinese porcelain with saucers adorned with golden spoons. He set them down and then turned and got the cream and sugar. I was impressed. He was dressed in a nice form-fitting suit. The shirt was stripped dobby, and the suit was a classic grey and made of linen. He had a straw hat hanging up and was sporting a very bright pink bowtie. His teeth gleamed all white, even though he drank coffee. This man was put together.

"That name sounds familiar."

"It should be, as you have at least three policies on my family," I said as I handed over my mother's life insurance policy.

He took it and unfurled it. He glanced at it and said, "Let me see here in the account receivables." He took a key from his pocket, unlocked it, opened a bottom drawer to his desk, and pulled out a thick green ledger. He flipped through it and found what he was looking for. "Here it is; we received a cash surrender request for $2500, which triggered the sale of the assets we had invested, which came to roughly $183.75; after expenses, a check was cut for $175 and mailed to your home."

"I see; however, I have a general question about life insurance."

"Ask way."

"If someone dies and the heirs request a redemption of the life insurance at full face value, would that trigger a cash surrender?"

"It most certainly should not. As they are two separate things."

"Do tell?"

"A cash surrender is when one has no more use for the policy and wishes to cash out what value and dividends are in the policy. So, one can expect the redeemed value to be a lot less than the actual face value of the policy by orders of magnitude."

"That's what I thought. So, can you please look at my momma's policy and see what the request says?"

He looked down at the policy and saw it was a redemption request. His face turned white, then red with embarrassment. "No. That can't be right."

"Is there a problem?" I asked sweetly.

"Give me just a moment. I'm sorry, my secretary hasn't made it in yet, so I'll have to go over to her desk and see what is amiss."

"Take your time. I have all day."

He got up, visibly disturbed. He strode over to her desk with a purpose and then returned to his desk, pulled out a big green bank book, and went through it. I could see that his face was starting to turn grey.

"Was an error made?"

"Several."

"Okay. Well, these things happen, and companies are not infallible. They make mistakes and are allowed to correct them. So, first things first. Can you pick up the phone there, call the head office, and get this straightened out today?"

"It might take a couple of days."

"Fine. Then let's get that started, and then I will move on to my next piece of business."

He nodded in assent and then picked up the phone. I added cream and sugar and daintily drank my coffee while he sweated and was transferred from department to department. After a few minutes, he asked, "Is it all right if I take this call in the back, as this might take a while?"

"Sure."

He got up with the phone and walked it back around the corner. I could see that the cord was long and intended to be used this way. Just then, I heard the sound of the bell at the door, and a very young and beautiful secretary came sneaking in. She was blonde-haired, blue-eyed, and drop-dead gorgeous. She had long legs that went all the way up to her neck, with magnificent round full bosoms and pouty lips. I could smell the scent of heavy perfume that was wearing in an attempt to cover up the smell of fresh sex. So, they were an item. Yeah, that made sense. She meekly looked at me and said, "I'm sorry. Have you been helped?"

"Yes, Jaimie's helping me."

"I'm Madeline."

'Of course, you would have a pretty girl's name,' I thought. Then, he said, "I'm Dorothy- Jane." Then I thought to myself, 'Wait, what just happened? Why do I see her as a threat?'

"That name sounds familiar."

"It should be since y'all recently wrote a check to my household."

She smiled sweetly and asked, “How did it go?”

“Not well.”

She looked puzzled, “Why not?”

“Because instead of redeeming my momma’s policy, wires got crossed; it was turned into a cash surrender.”

Her face fell and then went white. Their reactions were genuine, meaning they were consummate professionals and took this business very seriously—points in their favor. I can work with that.

She approached his desk and saw the ledger and the checkbook open. She visibly grimaced and then said, “Excuse me.”

“Certainly.”

She then went around the corner, and they conversed animatedly while whispering loudly. It was pretty cute, and I was enjoying the show. Finally, he hung up the phone with too much force and returned to his desk. He looked me dead in the eye and said, “Madame.”

“It’s Miss.”

“Miss, I must apologize. On behalf of myself and my staff, we have done you a disservice, and there is no excuse for the errors made on your mother’s estate.”

“Why don’t we all calm down and just walk me through your whole process so we can figure out what happened and where it happened and try to make sure that it doesn’t happen again.”

So, she pulled a chair up to the desk, and he laid it all out for me, “I won’t sugar coat it. So, once we receive the request for redemption, a copy is placed into an inter-office envelope and sent to the headquarters.”

“I suspected as much. So, at that point, it’s out of your hands?”

“In a manner of speaking, but we are still responsible for the policy’s disposition.”

“Noted. Continue.”

“Then, the proper department fills out the receivables request and orders the sale of the assets. Then they fill out a receipt and send it to us here at this office for processing.”

“Okay. Go on.”

“Then we write out the check and mail it to you.”

“Why would you do that here and not in the main office?”

“For speed of service. Since many policies are only several hundred dollars, we can write the check locally and get it into your hands quicker.”

“That makes sense. And I like the fact that you are willing to step up.”

They both sighed in relief.

I continued, “So, what is the redemption value of my mother’s policy?”

“ $2560.78”, he said.

“Okay. How long until corporate can send that out?”

“Several weeks.”

“And what are you offering me in return?”

“I can offer ten percent minus any amounts we have already paid. So, $81.08.”

“Try that math again.”

“Miss?”

I placed a copy of the deposit slip on his desk showing that the check cashed from his company was only $75.00. He compared it to his ledger and started to look a little ill. Then, he swallowed hard and said, "Noted."

"So, 181.08?"

"Yes, I do believe that is correct."

He was now starting to squirm. But I let him off of the hook. "Sounds great."

He bent over his checkbook, wrote out the check for the correct amount, compared it thrice, and had Madeline sign as well. He handed it to me, and I made a big show of placing it in my purse.

"You said that you had another request.", he said, looking twice as nervous and slightly guilty.

"Pshaw, this one's no trouble at all. My daddy took a policy out on me when I was born, and I want to know what I can do about it."

They both let out the breath that they were holding in.

He smiled back into true form, "That's what we call a conversion. Let me go and get your policy from the records room."

"I'll get it.", said Madeline as she got up quickly and retreated into the back.

"May I have a refill, please?" I asked, all sugar and spice. What I was doing went against form for me, but it wasn't his fault. Some twit elsewhere messed up everything. But it was something that could be fixed. Not right away, but they were making amends immediately. Once again, points in their favor.

About five minutes later, Madeline returned with a small card. It was attached to a copy of my birth certificate. It was yellowed and cracking with age, considering that it was almost eighteen years old.

He grabbed a form on the top of his in-out box and filled it out. After a few minutes, he asked me simple questions like, “Is your full name Dorothy-Jane….”

“Yes.”

“Do you own or will be attempting to own any other insurance policies?”

“No.”

“Are you married?”

“No.”

“What is your occupation?”

“Student. But I waitress part-time at the diner in Lake Tillery.”

He looked surprised by that, and Madeline gave him a sharp look. Then he shrugged and continued to ask questions, “Who is your next of kin?”

“That would be my brother Anthony.”

“Age?”

“Ten.”

They both asked at the same time, “Ten?”

“Affirmative.”

“Do you smoke?”

“No.”

“Drink alcohol?”

“No.”

“Have you ever been convicted of any felonies?”

“No.”

"Excellent. I will need $5.00 to pay the premium."

I reach into my purse and hand him the money, all in change. I take his receipt and say, "Thank you for your time." I rise from the chair, turn around, and walk out the door. My next stop will be the Bank of Troy, just around the corner, where I make the deposit. While I was at the window, I asked the teller, "May I see the bank manager, please?"

"Do you have an appointment?"

"No. I do not. I'm in town on business and need to clear up something." I said all bluster.

She seemed to think about this for a second and then thought about how I was dressed and the large amount of money I had just deposited into my account. That gave her the gumption to ask for a meeting immediately. As far as she knows, I'm some businesswoman with some clout. It's amazing that money talks, and you don't have to say a word. Just let it happen.

"I'll check for you. Please have a seat." She said, gesturing to the brown leather sofas in the lobby area.

After a few minutes, a well-dressed white male in his late fifties comes down the stairs and walks past a row of other male workers dressed in business suits. He looks at them like they should be working harder; to a man, they assume the position as they lean over their papers and get to work in earnest. He walks right up to me and offers his hand. "I'm sorry to keep you waiting, "Ms.?"

"Dorothy-Jane," I said in a crisp, business-like voice.

"Is there any reason that you need to see me?"

"Why don't we go to your office and see?" I said as I grabbed his arm, placed it in mine, and walked him up the stairs. At this point, I wanted to vomit, with all of this putting on airs, but it was powerful.

I never dreamed that the right woman, appropriately dressed and acting graciously, could achieve so much. Tarnation it was downright addictive. Now I know what they mean when people say, 'You have them wrapped around your finger.'

We arrive at his office, and he gets behind the desk and asks me, "What can I do for you?"

"I just have a question about the small life insurance policies that you have attached to people's accounts."

He visibly relaxed. I could see the wheels turning, but he thought, "Why am I getting involved?'

"Greg could better handle any normal questions…."

I can tell he can see right through me. He looked me up and down and saw that my Sunday best was a recut dress of momma ten years out of date. My shoes are simple, and my purse is worn while clean and cared for. No lady would dare have that on her person. He is done with me. This type of man only sees people who have money or clout. I'm neither. So, here comes the brushoff.

"I'm not asking Greg; I'm asking you."

"One moment." He opens a drawer and flips a switch. "Christine, could you come in for a moment?"

"Right away, sir."

A second or two later, she enters the room with a clipboard. She is a small, slight woman with a short haircut and wearing a grey sweater, navy blue shirt, and baby blue blouse with sensible brown shoes. "How may I help?"

"Can you escort this young lady to see Greg about an insurance policy?"

"Certainly.", she said and motioned for me to follow.

I turned back and said sweetly, “Thank you for your time.”, and waved. I could see the dark look on his face as he realized he had been hoodwinked. But that was fine by me. I was starting in this female manipulation stuff. I guess it doesn’t always work or give you the desired results.

We went down three flights of stairs into the boiler room. It was dank, and there was moisture everywhere.

She stopped us right in front of an office with a frosted pane window named Gregorios Samaras, spelled out in black letters. She knocked, and he responded, “It’s open.”

She struck her head in and said perfunctorily, “Greg, I’ve got a client that ended upstairs by mistake. Take care of her, please.”, she ordered as she lightly placed her hand in the small of my back and pushed me inside as she closed the door behind me.

“That woman has some skill,” I murmur.

I see that there are files stacked everywhere, and behind a desk is an office worker about 25 years old with an olive-skinned complexion and dark brown hair with slight curls. His hair is very shiny and glistens in the light. He is dressed in a plain white shirt and has a green lampshade bookies visor. He smiles at me, takes the visor off, and asks, “How may I help you, Ms.?”

“It’s Dorothy-Jane…..”

“And what is your question about insurance?”

“When an account holder has a policy with your institution, and they receive an associated Life Insurance Policy, how does one determine what amount will be there?”

“Well, it’s based on how many thousands of dollars are being held in trust by this bank for that person.”, he states matter of factly.

"What about if they don't have thousands just lying around? What is the absolute minimum that anyone will receive?"

"$250."

"Not $25."

"Not $25. Why do you ask?"

"Because my momma died a few weeks ago, and when we closed her account due to her death, we were told that she had a small policy for Life Insurance and we would receive the check in a few weeks."

"Any, you only got the $25?"

"Absotively."

He smirked and said, "Let me check on that."

I said quickly, "Oh, speaking of checks. Here is the one that your bank cut me." I said as I removed the deposit slip that had been validated.

He picked up the phone and asked to speak to the head of receivables.

A few minutes passed, and he said, "Okay. I'll check. Thanks"

He put the phone down and said, "Let me check the mailroom. I'll be right back.", he said as he got up and left the office. Five minutes later, he came back in smiling. He was holding a batch of envelopes in his hand. He sat down and opened one. He nodded and then handed it to me. "I think this is what you are looking for."

It was the check for the remainder of the money and a letter from the insurance company. It read:

To the family of …

With deep condolences, we send the funds your loved ones entrusted to us. As a part of the community, we have set up a way for everyone to obtain Life Insurance through The Bank of Troy, located at 301 N. Main St., Troy, NC, and even include it as a benefit in your accounts. Some are even available at no cost. The minimum is $250. Your family member had two accounts with us: a Checking account numbering 4567-3214A and a Passbook Savings account numbering 345-89067. Therefore, the total sum of $500 was exercised upon notification of their passing. Through a prearranged agreement, $250 was wired directly to Andersons Funeral home at 324 Hawk Crest Way, Lake Tillery, NC. A check for immediate expenses was sent directly to the address we have on hand. It was for 10% of the face value or $25.00. The corresponding check number was 347-456B-39B. Here is the check for the remainder of the funds. Enclosed Is check #545323-W-39A for the amount of $225.00.

Sincerely,

Weinman Weidman

DMK

"Will there be anything else, Miss?"

"No, thank you. I'll be on my way."

"If you want to deposit that, I can take care of it right here and save you the trouble of waiting in line."

"Do tell."

He smiles again and, with a flourish, produces a deposit slip. He quickly writes down our address and then asks me, do you know your account number?"

"I have it right here.", I say as I reach into my purse and produce my passbook savings account.

He takes it away from me, opens it to the first page, and notates the number. Then, he takes the check, writes that number on the back, and slides it to me.

“Please sign here.”, he states.

“Certainly. Oh, and one more thing, may I also withdraw $5.00?”

“Absolutely.”, he says as he pulls out another small book and begins to write on it. He then slides it to me. “Please sign here as well.”

I do, and then he takes all the paperwork and tucks it into a clear tube with a rotating black cover. He then slid open one of the pipes I thought was for heating and pressed a button at the bottom. There is a slight ‘whooshing’ sound as the tube engages.

He can tell that I’m perplexed by this contraption, so he explains. “This here is a pneumatic tube. It uses compressed air to send it to the teller station, where they will process the request. In a few minutes, they will return your receipts and the $5.00 you requested.”

“That’s neat. Amazing times we are living in.” Then I think to myself, ‘Is he flirting with me?’

“Well, this type of technology has existed since the late 1800s.”

“Really? Well, I declare.”, I said, using my best Sunday accent. ‘I guess it’s time to flirt back.’, I think.

He smirked, and then there was a ‘whooshing sound,’ and the tube returned. He opened up the pipe and withdrew the tube. He handed me my receipts, the passbook, and a crisp $5 bill.

“Is there anything else that I can do for you?”

“Can you suggest a good place for a light meal?”

“Well, there is the Automat.”

“What is that?”

"Oh, you've never heard of one. Then you are in for a treat. It is a vending machine for food."

My face told him I was very skeptical.

"I am getting ready to take a break. I'm not trying to be too forward, but I can escort you there and show you the principles.", he said carefully.

"That would be divine.", I agreed.

We both stood up, and he retrieved his jacket and hat from the coat rack behind the door. Then he exited his office and locked the door with a key. We walked up the stairs and went through a side lobby that opened up to street level. As we exited, bells clashed as a trolley turned the corner in front of us. 'Wow,' I thought, 'Delbert would hate this place. All the hustle and bustle would overpower his senses.' We walked about a block and a half and then went inside a modest-looking storefront with a Henderson & Merch's Automat sign. The glass had pictures of food and the prices listed. It was set up cafeteria style with all the tables and chairs in the center. The far back walls were lined with individual, glass-fronted compartments with a coin slot and a lever.

He instructed me in its use, "You just walk up to what you want and place the coin in the slot. Then pull on the lever, and the door opens up." He retrieved a ham sandwich on a plate with a transparent cover to keep the bread from going stale. He then walked over to another machine that had glasses on it. He obtained one and held it under a spigot. He slid two pennies into it, and a glass of milk came out. He walked everything over to a table and placed them there. He said, "And what would you like?" offering to pay. But I would have none of it.

“Thank you, kind sir, but I can get my own.” I could see that he was crestfallen, so I relented and gave him hope. “However, I will join you in just a minute.”

“As you wish,” he said, sitting down.

I walked over to the wall and gave a cursory glance, then, making my selection, slid a nickel into the slot and retrieved a BLT. Then, I walked down, picked up a tray from the service line, went to the desserts, got a slice of apple pie, walked over to the soda fountain, and got a root beer. I strode over to him, and he stood up as I approached the table. ‘Well, this boy has excellent manners,’ I thought.

As we were seated, he asked, “Miss, would you mind if I prayed before we ate?”

“Of course.”, I said as I bowed my head. I could hear him mumbling in some foreign language.

“Amen.”, he said.

“What was that?”

“Pardon?”

“That language that you just used.”

“Oh, that was Greek.”

“It sounds like music.”

“I’ve never thought of it like that.”, he said as he proceeded to cut up his sandwich with a fork and knife.

“Well, that’s unusual.”, I said.

“What is?”

“You’re cutting up your sandwich and eating it with a fork and knife.”

“Really?”

“I’ve never thought about it.”, he said as he carefully lifted the fork to his mouth and ate the morsel. He nodded to say, ‘Why don’t you try it?’

I took my fork and knife and attempted to do the same. The results were downright pitiful. The blade scraped the plate in a shrieking sound. People looked up at the audible assault. After hacking at it, I finally got a bite to my lips, but the bacon fell off and tumbled down to the plate.

“Maybe that sandwich was not the best for eating in this way. But my parents are from Europe, which is how we eat everything.”

I gave up, put down the fork and knife, and picked up the sandwich with my hands. “Sorry, I gave it a try, but I don’t think I am cultured enough to do it well or even at all. I guess I’m just a provincial girl “, I said as I took a bite of my sandwich.

He nodded. “I think it would take some experimentation, and maybe next time, try it with a turkey or ham.”

“Nah. I’m good. But I do have another question.”

“What is it?”

“Why do you use your utensils backward?”

“I’m not sure what you mean by that.”

“Well, lookie here.”, I said as I picked up my fork and knife with the fork on the left and the blade on the right.

“Yes, but you don’t cut your meat with it that way. You start correctly and then reverse everything.” He demonstrated. We cut it and pick it up to our mouths, but you fumble about and switch hands.”

“Most people are right-handed, but we are trained to cut with our left hand. Come to think of it, I’m not entirely sure. I’ll have to get back to you on that one.”

“Please do.”, he said hopefully.

“I have another question.”, I asked.

“Ask away.”

“What does your last name mean?”

“It means saddle maker. Why do you ask?”

“I’ve just never seen that kind of name before. But it makes sense, as your clothing is expertly tailored.”

“Thank you. It is, after all, the family business., he said modestly.

“Why didn’t you go into it?”

“My father wanted a better life for me. Hence, why we moved here to this country.”

A few minutes later, we completed eating, and I told him, “I would like to thank you for the courtesy that you have shown me. But I must be on my way. I hope I did not cause you to be late for work.”

He smiled and made a dismissive gesture with his hand. “It’s wonderful. How often do you get into town?”

“About once a month or so.”

“Well then, I hope to see you next month, and hopefully, you will have an answer about that fork and knife etiquette.”

I blushed slightly and responded, “Maybe.” I had never met anyone that wasn’t black or white. Here was a handsome man who was olive-skinned. There was a whole world out there that I hadn’t even seen yet. I guess that was what old Wilford was trying to tell me, and I wasn’t listening.

We took our trays to these baker racks and placed them on them. I then walked out. I left a nickel as a tip on my tray for whoever had to clean up after us. For heaven's sake, I would be out of a job shortly if this were the future. But then again, this was a big city where everyone hurried to get things done and move on to the next thing. I don’t think it would work in Lake Tillery because people stopped off for the meal, gas, and water.

He went on his way, and I mine. I got to thinking, as I had never really had the opportunity to see Troy properly. The express bus wouldn’t be ready to leave for a while, so I decided to be a tourist.

Fork and Knife Etiquette

I wandered around Troy and noticed their lovely parks and lush trees. I also noticed that the park was full of men. They were sitting on benches, and some were lying in the grass with despondent looks on their faces. They looked like they had been beaten like harp seals. I guess it's a real blow to a man's ego to lose his job and everything else that goes along with it. I saw a lady dressed in a military uniform stopping by each one and offering them comfort. Be it a cold drink of water, a piece of fruit, or a sandwich. She had a basket that contained all of these items. There was a red lock box with a coin slot at the top, and the words 'Donations Accepted' were painted in white. I reached into my purse, got out a quarter, and dropped it into the slot. She looked at me and said, "Thank you, miss." I could now see that her uniform bore the Salvation Army's crest. She reached into her basket, pulled out a tract, and handed it to me, stating, "We can always use volunteers."

I said, "Thank you, but I'm from out of town."

She replied, "We have chapters everywhere. God bless you."

Tears came to my eyes as I left. Here was an Angel of Mercy, ministering to the downtrodden and offering them hope. It was in small ways, but at least it was something. Collectively, this country could do great things, but President Woodrow Wilson was a self-made man who decided that when the economy took a downturn, he would do nothing to intervene. It was the little man's problem, and he should rely on himself. He let those men at the top who controlled the stock market take away all of their money and rode those companies into the dust. The effects were long-lasting and detrimental to the nation as a whole. People were committing suicide left and right over this, and we as a country were in a death spiral.

I guess that's why he was now out of a job, and the population took risks in electing Franklin Delano Roosevelt. He was the Governor of New York State from 1929 to 1932, served as the Assistant Secretary of the Navy from 1913 to 1920, and was a member of the New York State Senate from 1911 to 1913. He had a pretty good pedigree; as the governor of New York, he had implemented many programs to combat the Great Depression to see if he was up to the task of caring for the nation. The people voted, and he won by a landslide. Everyone was optimistic.

I walked away and found the library. I strode up the steps and found the card catalog. I copied down the Library of Congress Numerical system to the correct section. I found a book on Etiquette and table manners and began to read. It was entitled Ms. Manners-Guide to Etiquette in our current era.

It contained all the usual stuff on being a great hostess at a party. But there was also a section about entertaining foreign visitors/guests. The section began: When engaging in a cosmopolitan area, one might have the pleasure of having a guest from an unfamiliar part of the world arrive. As a hostess, you must ensure that all guests feel comfortable. Table manners differ in certain parts of the world, and dietary restrictions must be honored. For example, In Ethiopia and the Middle East, people eat with their right hand from a communal bowl. In Asia, people use chopsticks, and when entering a home, they remove their shoes. If you are entertaining an Asian guest, you might ask that your other guests bring slippers or go without shoes while at the party. It could be a nice change of pace for everyone.

European table manners are quite different as well. They will hold the fork in their left hand and cut with the knife in their right. The fork typically faces downwards and is only curved up as it reaches your mouth. Europeans usually tend to linger at the table and enjoy multiple courses.

American diners hold the fork in the left hand and the knife in the right. Then, they placed the knife on the plate and switched the fork to the right hand. Americans will never put food into their mouth while holding a knife.

The main reason for this harkens back to the American Revolution. Food was eaten communally at large tables when the populace was more rustic. The tavern/public house would only provide spoons and forks as eating utensils. Most men provided their own knives. Therefore, since most people are right-handed, a new rule called the tavern rule insisted that you cut the meat with your right and switch the fork over. This leaves the knife on the plate, and if there are any disagreements over politics, rudeness, etc., both parties are not armed at first and must reach down to retrieve their knife. This means that no one person would have the upper hand.

I thought about it. It made sense. I wrote my observations on paper and wrote Greg's name on the front. And put the book in the return cart. I walked back towards the bank and found a pneumatic massage tube. I placed the message inside the tube and hoped it would reach Greg. I pressed the button, which shot off a 'whooshing' sound.

I thought I had just deposited $406.08 minus the $5. That left 401.08, plus the $100, so $501.08. That ought to be enough to take care of the taxes owed on the property. I could breathe a little easier.

Once the remainder came in from Life of Virginia, that would leave us with $2800. An excellent monthly salary for a worker was $30 a month. So that would give us reserves for about 7.75 years. If I quit working tomorrow, we would have enough to live on until he turned 18. But I would always work. It was in my nature.

Inauguration Day

It's March 4th and Inauguration Day. The town is decked out in red, white, and blue bunting. We have the day off of school for the event. It seems like the entire population is snuggled up in the diner, listening to the radio. Shelby unplugged the jukebox and flipped it around. He even put a 'Broken' sign on it to hush up anybody who wanted to complain. This was too important. Since it was all grey and rainy outside, Shelby put coffee and hot tea at ½ price and free hot chocolate for the children if the parents ordered a slice of pie. He was busy making his famous chili, and there was plenty of cornbread to go with it. He had us ladling the cold batter into cast iron trays with little corn ears as a mold. He even ordered extra milk because his chili was spicy, and the milk would help cut the heat. He was always mindful of his customers and, knowing that times were hard, came up with plenty of ways to ensure that everyone could at least get a decent meal, no matter how little they had.

He devised a campaign called 'The Angel Fund.' Anyone could pay for a meal, coffee/milk, tea, or any other beverage, a bowl of soup, or a sandwich. The cost would be written on a slight angle cutout. These would then be placed in the register on the side of the till opposite the large bills. A small sign at the register said, 'Angel Meals: Ask your server about it.' We tended to get many people through here. Traveling salesmen on business, truckers, and families that stopped off for gas and a meal on their way elsewhere.

We listened to the radio as the motorcade started. The announcer started up,

Former President Woodrow Wilson and President-Elect Franklin Delano Roosevelt had just climbed into the car to take them down Pennsylvania Ave to the White House. (The crowd is cheering in the background.) Wilson does not look very comfortable, but FDR is gleaming with pride. The chief Justice Charles Hughes performs the swearing-in, 'You, Franklin Delano Roosevelt, Do solemnly swear that you will faithfully execute the Office of President of the United States and will, to the best of your ability, preserve, protect and defend the Constitution of the United States, so help you, god?'

'I, Franklin Delano Roosevelt, do solemnly swear that I will faithfully execute the office of President of the United States and will preserve, protect, and defend the Constitution of the United States, so help me god. President Hoover, Mr. Chief Justice, my friends. This is a day of National Consecration. And I am certain that on this day, my fellow Americans expect that on my induction into the Presidency, I will address them with candor and a decision with the present situation….this great nation will endure as it has endured and will prosper. First, let me firmly believe that the only thing we have to fear is fear itself. Nameless, unreasoning, unjustified terror. Which paralyzes needed efforts to convert retreat into advance…Taxes have risen, our ability to pay has fallen…the means of exchange are frozen. ….Farmers find no market for their produce, and the savings of many years and thousands of families are gone. More importantly, many unemployed citizens face the grim problem of existence, and an equally great number toil with little return. Only a foolish optimist will deny the realities of the moment…..Primarily, this is because the rulers of the exchange of mankind's goods have failed through their stubbornness and their incompetence and have admitted their failures and abdicated.

Practices of the unscrupulous money changers stand indicted in the court of public opinion…True, they have tried, but their efforts have been cast in the pattern of an outworn tradition….. Faced with the failure of credits, they have proposed only lending more money…. They have resorted to extortion…they only know the rules of a generation of self-seekers. They have no vision, and the people perish without vision. Yes, the money changers have fled from their high seats in the temple of our civilization. We may restore that temple..(applause)…. Restoration calls, however, not for changes in ethics alone; this nation is asking for action and action now. (applause and stamping of feet)

Our greatest primary task is to put people to work (applause). This is no unsolvable problem if we face it wisely and courageously. It can be accomplished in part by directly recruiting the government itself, treating the task as we treat the emergency of a war. But at the same time, through this employment, we accomplish greatly needed projects to stimulate and reorganize the use of our great natural resources. Hand in Hand with them, we must frankly recognize the overbalance of population in our industrial centers and by engaging on a national scale in a redistribution endeavor to provide a better use of the land for those best fitted for the land…..It can help by realistically preventing the tragedy of the growing loss through foreclosure of our small homes and farms. It can be helped by insisting that the federal, state, and local governments act forthwith on the demands that their costs be drastically reduced. It can be supported by unifying relief activities, which are often scattered, uneconomical, and unequal today. It can be supported by national planning for and supervision of all forms of transportation, communications, and other utilities that have a public character. There are many ways in which it can be helped. But it can never be supported by merely talking about it. (Applause) We must act, we must act quickly, and finally, in our progress towards the resumption of work, we require two safeguards against a return of the evils of the old order. There must be strict supervision of all banking, credits, and investments. There must be an end to speculation with other people's money. There must be a provision for an adequate but sound currency.

These, my friends, are the lines of attack. I shall presently enlist upon a new congress in special session detailed measures for their fulfillment, and I shall seek the immediate assistance of the help of the 48 states.

Through this program of action.. we shall be putting our own national house in order and making income balance outgo….. I am prepared under my constitutional duties to recommend the measures that a stricken nation amid a stricken world may require. These measures or such other measures as the congress may bill out of its experience and wisdom. I shall seek within my constitutional authority to bring to speedier done, but if the congress fails to take one of these two courses. If the national emergency is still critical, I shall not evade the clear course of duty that will then confront me. I shall ask Congress for the remaining instrument to meet the broad executive power crisis. Wage war against the emergency as great as the power given to me if a foreign foe invaded us. (applause)

Shelby said, "Well, now I think that about covers it."

"Time will tell.", I said.

Home Economics

I had signed up for Home Economics in school right after momma got sick. The first part of the class was all about the business side of running a household. Making budgets, paying bills, and the like. But this week, we were getting into the fun stuff, the actual art of cooking. We started with braised beef. Mrs. Maxwell's teacher was a very thin, prim, and proper woman. She always addressed us as 'ladies' and kept ignoring that Geoff Watkins was present. I asked him, "Why are you here?"

"So, I don't get ptomaine poisoning, Dot."

"No."

"Uh, because this is where all of the girls are at. Plus, when I go to college, maybe I can impress a date."

"Not a bad plan."

"So, do you want to be partners?"

"Why not?"

"Okay, then what do you want to do first?" he asked

"Why don't you start with the meat, and I'll get the rest of the ingredients out of the pantry."

"Sounds like a plan."

He got all the bowls, a cutting board, a knife, and the packet of meat wrapped in butcher paper.

I came back with the various ingredients.

He looked down at the instructions and was a little perplexed.

“What is it?” I asked.

“It says to wash it under water and remove the membrane and inspection stamp?”

“Hold on; I think I remember something about that in the text.” I rummage around and find it. I flip it around and show him. “See how it describes a whiteish, almost clear membrane.”

“Okay.” He says as he grabs the meat and starts to pinch it, and we both can see the membrane. He tries to hack at it with the chef's knife, to no avail. I quickly grab a fruit knife and have a go at it. I easily slide the knife under the membrane and break its contact with the meat. He then steps in and peels it back into one full sheet. We can all hear him ripping it away from the muscle. He has a sheet about eight inches long and twenty-four inches wide.

“First obstacle down.” I look at the other students, and they are perplexed with the assignment; they are in various stages of preparation, and not a single one has completed the first task. I knew we were being graded on how well we followed directions and timed how long it took us to prepare this meal.

“It says to trim the fat, then render it and to cut the meat into cubes.”, he says

“Okay, so?”

“So, what does that mean?”

“It means,” I said, picking up the correct knife for the job, ”To cut the excess fat off,” I said, showing him how to trim it. I placed a cast iron skillet on the gas stove and threw the excess fat into the pan.

“To cube it means to cut the meat into strips about this long and then cut them into cubes about this big. The cubes measured out to be about two inches on each side.” I returned the knife, and he made short work of the meat.

In no time, I had taken the meat, dropped it into the flour, pulled it out, and placed it onto a plate. Then, once we had enough fat rendered, I put these dusted morsels into the pan and lightly browned them on each side. We used a wooden spoon to stir them. While I was managing the meat, he was prepping the vegetables. We had two potatoes, each about the size of a fist, one medium-sized carrot, one small onion, one-fourth of a medium-sized turnip, and one celery stalk. He cut the veggies in a general manner with absolutely no finesse.

While working, the teacher lectured us, “Class, good beef should be bright red, moist, and juicy. When freshly cut, the muscle should be firm and have a fine grain to it. The fat should be about an inch or so thick. This serves two purposes. One is to give you enough to render, but the fat also has much flavor and satisfies. Why do you think that we like gravy so much? It’s because it is made of the drippings of meat. Also, remember to buy enough meat for each person, as meat tends to shrink from one-third to one-half during cooking. Therefore, allow one-fourth of a pound of meat without bone for each serving. The less expensive cuts come from the neck and shank for stews and boiling. With proper care and preparation, one can take a tough piece of meat and boil it down until it is tender enough to be eaten with a spoon.”

I looked at the sad pile of vegetables murdered for the cause and grimaced. As I placed the meat in the pressure cooker, I said to him, "Geoff, we are going to need to practice on your knife work."

He let out an exasperated sigh, "I know. But since it's a stew, maybe she won't notice."

We looked at the sheet, added the seasoning and spices, and covered it with the obligatory two cups of beef stock. Then I wrestled with the seal, turned it right, and locked it into place. We then made sure to fold the lever that married the two handles together and placed the small silver safety ball on top. Geoff then picked up the pot and put it on the stove. We turned the gas up high and set the timer.

The next step was to prepare a pot of rice to go with the stew. Seeing the difficulty of a simple task, Mrs. Maxwell asked Geoff and me to prepare six rice cuts in a large pot. I showed him how to run the pot under the sink water and drop the rice in.

Mrs. Maxwell saw me and asked, "Why Dorothy-Jane, whatever are you doing?" She didn't realize it, but she clutched her pearls around her neck as she said it.

"Just washing the rice, ma'am."

"What?"

"It's just something that a Chinese Missionary wife taught my momma. You wash the rice several times to remove the hull remnants and extra starch. It should be done until the water is clear. It can take up to six times. The best way to do this is to let it settle overnight. Kind of like washing beans."

So, I proceeded to show her what I knew. Once we had washed enough, we added the right proportion of water and placed it on the stove next to the pressure cooker. We covered it and set another timer.

Mrs. Maxwell was surveying the other students and seeing that almost all had placed the ingredients into the pressure cooker. She exclaimed, “Oh dear, this isn’t going well.”

We could hear the slight whistling as the other pressure cookers started up. There was a bit of a rolling boil noise to the whole affair.

“Geoff and Dot, since we have about half an hour before any of these dishes will be ready, do you think you two could manage to start on a batch of cookies?”

“What kind, ma’am?” I asked.

“Sugar Cookies as they take the least amount of time. Page 187”, she declared absently as she rushed off to avert a disaster. “Mabel, did you put any soup stock in that? She says as she grabs a large bath towel, removes the offender from the stove, and rushes it to the sink. There is a black cloud escaping the pressure cooker. She covers it in the towel and instructs everyone, “In the case of a mishap, this is the safest place for the pressure cooker.” She reached into her apron and pulled out a timer. Don’t anyone come here nor touch it until this timer dings? Get it?”

The whole class responded in unison, “Got it.”

“Good: she replied and then strode down the aisle, with a clipboard in hand surveying the damage and how well or poorly everyone followed directions.

Meanwhile, Geoff and I were working on the bonus assignment. We gathered the shortening, sugar, eggs, flour, baking powder, milk, salt, and vanilla. We had brown sugar, and the vanilla was a whole bean. I read the directions to Geoff since he seemed not to understand them anyway. “Cream the shortening and mix well with the sugar.”

“What?”

"Beat the damn thing with a whisk and add the brown sugar."

"Now, separately beat the two eggs and add them to the main mixing bowl."

"Ok. Why did we do that separately?"

"I dunno. Write it down and ask later."

So, he wrote the questions down on an index card.

"Now take all of the dry ingredients and mix them in a separate bowl."

He did so and said, "Done. Next."

Now add the dry ingredients to the main bowl in halves."

"You lost me."

"Pour half of the dry mix into the main bowl."

"Done."

"Now add half of the milk and stir all ingredients together."

Ok."

"Now alternate the remaining ingredients to the main bowl."

"Wow. That's a lot of different steps for a pretty plain cookie."

"Okay, now let's trade places as I know you'll just futz this up."

I got out the rolling pin and cutting board. I dusted it with flour and dumped the pastry onto the board. I then rolled it out until it was ¼ inch thick, grabbed the cookie cutters, and started cutting them. We then placed them onto a greased baking sheet. I lifted the dough, squashed it together again, then rolled it out again, and this time, I used the gingerbread man cutter. Those went onto a separate greased baking sheet, and we dusted them with sugar and put them into a preheated oven at 375 degrees for 10 minutes.

Geoff went over to the pressure cooker and shut off the fire. He then waited about three minutes, and using a towel, he carefully pulled at the little ball on the top of the pressure cooker. It shrieked like a banshee as steam escaped from the top. This startled some of the girls. The second timer went off, and he pulled the rice off the stove and moved it to the chopping block. He always ensured he used a towel or a potholder when he came into contact with any hot piece of metal. At least he was following the safety instructions. There was reading, and there was comprehension. I know he was good at both but was never allowed into the kitchen, whereas I grew up in one. I had observed all of the women folk for years. So, I couldn't be too hard on him. At least he was trying; we were here to learn.

I got busy arranging the twenty-one bowls we would need to serve all the disasters.

Now that the shrieking had stopped, he grabbed a towel, threw it over the pressure cooker, and carefully turned each handle in the opposite direction. There was a slight plop, and some vapor escaped. He removed the towel, went to the cast iron pan, and removed all the meat using tongs. He then put the vegetables into the pressure cooker and put them back together. Next, he placed it back onto the stove and put the ball back on top. He set the timer for 15 minutes, and before we knew it, the sugar cookies were done.

Next, he repeated the steps with the pressure cooker and dumped everything back into the skillet. He cranked the fire up to medium, and I got the corn starch and water ready. When it came to a boil, we added the mixture carefully while stirring, and there you have it—braised Beef Stew.

Mrs. Maxwell just shook her head in disbelief. "Well, ladies and you, good sir. It seems that we have our first dish ready."

"Dorothy-Jane, you may serve the rice and Geoff the stew."

Each girl grabbed a bowl and got a spoonful of rice from me and a ladle of stew from him. They looked at the meager portion and were reminded by Mrs. Maxwell, “Now remember, girls, this is just a taste as we have over ten, well make that nine dishes. Before we partake, I believe a prayer is in order.”

We all bowed our heads, and she led us in prayer, “Dear heavenly father. We are thankful that you are watching over us and that there have been and will continue to be zero injuries. May you guide our hands as we prepare the food to nourish our bodies and those of our loved ones? Amen.”

“Amen .”, we all said in unison.

We then dug in. All in all, it was all right. “I think it needs a little hot sauce,” I said.

“I’ll get it.”, says Mabel as she dashed off to the pantry and returned with some.

Then, Mrs. Maxwell had each set of students finish their preparations. Two more were rejected outright as she deemed them unfit for consumption. She was right as four cooks managed to turn that bright pink meat into grey flotsam. The rest of the meals were tough as the girls either failed to remove the membrane, brown the beef, or both. All of the vegetables had disintegrated in everyone else’s dishes. She then let us wash our mouths out with milk and sugar cookies. She told the rest of the girls to do the washing up and told us to grab out things and meet her outside in the hallway. She looked at both of us and said, “Out of all of the students, I didn’t expect this of you.”

“What do you mean?”

“You’ve both impressed me, and that is hard to do. How did you do it?”

Geoff said, “Ma’am, it appears that cooking and chemistry are similar. Follow the directions, methods, and proportions, and everything will be fine.”

I just shrugged, “I’m not much of a cook. I never had to do much besides boil potatoes and make rice. But since my momma got ill, I really need to learn how to cook.”

“You both will receive the only A’s in the classroom and are excused. You may go home.”

“Is that fair?”

“If they had followed directions and not wasted the resources, they would not be in this mess, and they made a royal mess of my kitchen. I will see you both tomorrow. Your time is now your own. Good day.” She said as she handed us our passes to check out of school early.

We both looked at each other and shrugged.

Geoff congratulated me as we walked down the hall, “Well, Dot. It looks like we make a pretty great team.”

“That’s not saying much.”

“What do you mean.”

“The competition is not very stiff.”

“Well, we are students, after all.”

“True. I’m off to the Diner.”

“Why are you always working?”

“Because my momma died, and I’ve got a ten-year-old brother to look after.”

“I thought he was with the sheriff and his wife.”

“He is, but I still have a household to run, and there is Delbert.”

“What about him?”

“He needs looking after since his momma is ill. Don’t say what I think you’re gonna say.”

“I was just going to say, see you tomorrow.”, he replied as he dejectedly went down the hall to his locker.

I knew he drove a real rice sporty-looking roadster, and he was trim enough with all those track and field events he was going to. He was just lonely and needed a girl. The main problem with that was Geoff had moved to the area from Raleigh when we were about twelve, and everyone had paired up, and in this farming community, boys outnumbered girls. I guess that was just nature’s way of providing for what was needed. His daddy was a mill manager in New London, and his mother worked for a charity that dealt with indigent people. Well, as good-looking as he was, I just wasn’t interested in him. I only had a place in my heart for Delbert. Most people wouldn’t understand this. I had plenty of boys ask me why. And my reply was always the same, “The heart wants what the heart wants.”

Most of them were respectful and left me alone after that. Some idiots pressed the issue. I told them all the same thing, “I don’t suffer fools.” That was their only warning. I would drop any one of them if necessary. I even carried a roll of nickels all taped up in my purse. When I was at work, it was in my left apron pocket. If I was ever questioned about why I had them, the answer at school or in public was, this is my bus fare. At work, it was here’s spare change for the register. Since I was left-handed, it was readily available, and no male ever expected to be punched by a girl. I have laid quite a few out in my short little life span. Even if they were unconscious, their friends would drag them off. There was never any retaliation because the shame of being bested by a girl was too much for their fragile male egos.

Headlines for March 1933

March 9th, 1933, Lebanon Register, Lebanon, Kentucky Cost 5 cents

Federal Emergency Relief Act: The first action by the president of the United States was to have congress pass a bill that established the Federal Emergency Relief Act. This measure calls for spending $500,000,000 to provide relief to the poor. In the form of several measures. To provide soup kitchens in areas of high unemployment, blankets, and nursery schools for mothers who need to renter the workforce. It plans to offer employment to over 500,000 women.

Emergency Banking Act: The second proviso by the president is the Emergency Banking Act. This will provide safeguards and protection for deposits, which will be federally insured up to an aggregate amount of $5,000.

Bills in the works: Cullen-Harrison Act would repeal the Volstead act and allow for the sale, distribution, and consumption of beer with an alcohol content of up to 3.2%.

I put the paper down. This one had traveled a long way from Kentucky. I asked Shelby, "Hey, Shelby, they are getting ready to repeal the Volstead Act."

"Well, I be damned."

"What do you think about that?"

"I think I'll have a beer.", he said, laughing. "When will it happen?"

"It's going on right now. It just needs to be ratified."

"I think I'll call the distributor in Troy and have a chat."

"Good thinking."

The Burnsville Eagle Vol 40. No.18

March 20, 1933

The Act of March 20, 1933, is an Act of Congress that cut the salaries of federal workers and reduced benefit payments to veterans; these perfunctory moves were intended to reduce the federal deficit in the United States.

In other news, since the Emergency Banking Act passing, banks have seen a rise in deposits as those hoarding money are now returning it to the banks to be placed back into the economy. They now have a measure of faith that the full faith and credit of the United States Government would protect their money. Also, since the act, trading on the stock exchange has increased.

The Albemarle Sentinel

March 31, 1933

The Establishment of the Emergency Conservation Work (ECW) is designed to put young unmarried men to work. They must be able-bodied and between the ages of 18 and 25. This Army of young men will supply manual labor for conserving and developing natural resources. They will mainly help build infrastructure in Federal Parks and Federal Reserve Lands. The projected projects for the immediate area are fire towers and the building of the Blue Ridge Parkway. This roadway will connect North Carolina, Virginia, and Tennessee. There will be scenic overlooks, rest stops, and picnic areas. This will be a toll-free area. Many bridges and tunnel projects are incorporated along the route, which will take many years to complete. The ECW will erect a series of temporary camps in the area. We are moving them from place to place on an as-needed basis.

Op-Ed: Do we think these programs are good for the country? Do we think that Franklin Delano Roosevelt is the savior? Do we believe that Communism is the way to go? It is too soon to tell, as he has been in office for a short time. But he has surrounded himself with a cabinet of people striving to make inroads into the country's main problems. These problems have been going on for years and might take years to fix. But time marches on, and every little bit helps. As the Chinese say, 'Even one grain of rice can tip the scale.' Maybe we can tip the scales of our fortunes for the better.

Ronald Etwilder

Reading these cast-off papers was enlightening. Everyone seemed to have an opinion about what was happening. And they were so hungry for change that they were willing to see what would happen.

The Federal Government was putting people to work with massive Public Works Projects. But since most people here were farmers, ranchers, in the timber industry, and the like, we were fine. The President kept the promise he made to the people on inauguration day. To put people back to work. Life in those camps must be hard. However, they got paid. I heard they earned $30 a month, and $25 was sent directly home to their families. But they got three hots and a cot. In this day and age, that would have to be enough.

I had to admire the President. That man had a lot of chutzpah. But like he said in the inaugural address, the men in charge needed vision. They did what they always did, and the nation went down the drain. At least he was putting people to work and reintegrating money into the economy. In class one day, the teacher talked about a timber industry worker who gets paid $1.00. He is likely to spend it on meals, rent, gasoline, purchasing groceries, newspapers, movie tickets, etc. Then, everywhere he spends the money, they will use those funds to do the same. That $1.00 can bounce around in the economy up to 20 times. If the money is hoarded, it goes nowhere and doesn't add anything to the nation's buying power.

It can go far if that $1.00 is deposited in a bank. Since the bank will loan 90% of that money out, fueling the economy. So, let's say that a logging company gets a loan for new equipment. When they make that purchase, the salesman gets paid, and then he goes on to use that money to pay his rent, buy groceries, gas, sundry items, newspapers, have his shoes shined, and pay club membership dues. Money works well if it stays in the economy.

That was what the president was trying to do. Get the money moving in the economy again. The more people spent, the better off we all were because spending money helps generate tax revenue, which can then be used to fund projects at the Federal, State, and local level. Everyone plays, and everyone wins.

I Want a Coca-Cola

It was April, and I was thinking back to when Anthony was in a mood right after Momma died, and we were walking to the store to get some supplies, and he started up. I was lost in my thoughts, trying not to grieve, putting up a good front for Anthony.

"Dorothy-Jane?"

"Yes, Anthony?"

"I want a Coca-Cola."

"That's nice."

"No. I mean it. I want a Coca-Cola."

"Anthony.." I began, but he started crying.

"I WANT A COCA-COLA!!!!" he shrieked.

I turned to him, "Anthony. Anthony!!! Calm down! Stop it!" I said, tears in my eyes.

He looked at me and sobbed, "I want a Coca-Cola."

"I know, I know.", I said as I hugged him tight. "I miss her too."

We stood there for a minute, held each other, and then resumed walking to the store. "Okay, Anthony, we only have so much money. But if you want that Coca-Cola, you will have to earn it."

"How? I'm ten."

Spotting something shiny reflecting off in the bushes by the roadside, I pointed at it, smiling, "Like that."

He looked perplexed, "Like what?"

"Do you see that bottle over there?"

"Yeah.", he said carefully.

"Go over and pick it up."

He did and came back with it. "Now, see a price marked at the end."

"I do."

"Great. That is called a deposit. This one is for one cent."

"So?"

"So, a small bottle of Coca-Cola costs five cents. Find four more like this one, and you can have your Coca-Cola."

He did. We made a game of it. We put them in the momma's shopping bag made from a rice sack. When we got to the grocery store, we went to the front and got a receipt for eight cents. When we were done shopping, we treated ourselves to soda. He earned his Coca-Cola, and I got myself a Sunburst Cola for three cents. I got some fresh peaches and plenty of rock salt as we were going to make ice cream tonight.

I love homemade ice cream. The machine is quite simple; there is a wooden bucket that you insert a metal can. Then, you load up fresh fruit, syrup, sugar, and cream. Just fill it about 2/3 of the way, as the ice cream needs room to expand. Then, put the dashers into contact with the can and place the lid on top. Then, you set the crank over it and lock it into place. Then, you turn the crank over and over. This churns the heavy cream, and after about 30 minutes to an hour of hard cranking, you should get ice cream. It's a good thing that Delbert is strong. Anthony had a turn on the crank, but it only lasted a few minutes. The whole thing is chemistry. The ice and rock salt form a suspension fluid that can get really cold. This helps turn the cream into a frozen treat. Sitting at the table, all smiles as we enjoyed the hard-earned ice cream, got me thinking of the second day of cooking in the Home Economics class.

We arrived, and Mrs. Maxwell said, "Class, today we will try to do something more manageable. I've got cards here that have ten different recipes. Dot and Geoff, you may go first.

We got Snicker Doodles. Mabel got bread pudding, Charlotte got caramel custard, etc.

Our recipe was the same as the Sugar cookie but dusted with cinnamon. It was very disappointing. And Mrs. Maxwell could tell. "Whatever is wrong, dear?" she asked.

"There's no Snickers in this doodle."

Everyone laughed at the joke. Generally, I didn't like to be laughed at. But this was them laughing with me versus at me. Even Mrs. Maxwell was laughing. "Well, Dorothy-Jane, you are full of surprises. Geoff, why don't you head down to the school store and get us a few of them there Snickers bars," she said, handing him a quarter. That was enough for five bars.

He got up and left. Then she asked me, "So how will we prepare these Snickers Doodles?"

"Now that you ask, I'm not sure."

"Well, think about it. You have until he gets back."

A few minutes later, Geoff returned triumphantly. He dumped the four bars onto the butcher's block. She ignored the fact that one was missing. We decided as a class that we would try them four ways.

Mabel suggested, “Why don’t we just chop the snicker bar into pieces and incorporate it into the cookie? Then bake and see how it comes out.”

“That’s an excellent idea,” Mrs. Maxwell said as she wrote the suggestion on the board. “Who is next?”

Charlotte replied, “ Melt the bar and pour that over the cookie dough.”

“I don’t see why not. Go ahead and grab what you need. But remember to look up the directions on chocolate as it can be tricky.”

I came up with the next idea, “Let’s slice them real thin and lay them over top of the cookies.”

“Excellent idea. Go gather what you need.”

Mabel came up with the last idea, ”Let’s make the cookie and then, using a cheese grater, grate the confection over the cookies as they came out of the oven.”

Mrs. Maxwell thought about it by pursing her lips and finally consented. “It seems a bit crude but might be effective. After all, we are experimenting. There will be no grading today as this is supposed to be a fun exercise.”

We all visibly relaxed. So, we all had our projects. And once they were done, she eyed each one carefully.

Mabel’s project was first. They looked like dirty little snowmen but tasted okay.

Charlotte’s cookies came next. They had hardened up and looked like a hot mess but were fine.

Geoff and I were the next ones to be judged, and tasted like what I thought a snickerdoodle would taste like. Even Mrs. Maxwell thought the same, “Dorothy-Jane, now I see why you were so disappointed. Comparatively speaking, the Snickerdoodle tastes bland in comparison.”

Mabel’s was dead last and tasted fine.

“Well, class, what have we learned today?”

“That the price for running an errand is one snicker bar.”, said Charlotte.

Geoff’s face turned red.

“Come now, there was more than enough product left over.”, Mrs. Maxwell said, pointing to the remaining candy bars.”

18 at Last

The next thing I know is that it's May, and my 18th birthday is here. Wilford and Clara have a party, and he takes me down to the Electric Company to change everything to my name.

The manager greeted me businesslike and said, "Welcome to the co-op. I'm Mr. George."

"What do you do here, Mr. George?"

"I'm in charge of new accounts."

"So, is that all that you do all day?"

"No. There are accounting and collections duties as well as T-accounts."

"I see. Well, I have filled out my application. Here you go."

He collects it from me and gives it a once over. Excellent. Everything appears to be in order. I'll need to collect a deposit of $3.00."

I hand him the funds. $3.00. That's a real piece of irony.

He says, "We have a work order for a workman to be out at your place, and he will ensure that it's turned on no later than 4 p.m. Here are some brochures and pamphlets about electrical safety. Also, as a token of our gratitude, please accept this humble gift of a toaster.", he says, beaming with pride.

I think to myself. 'Why would I need to plug this in to get toast? We make toast on the stove at home. We have a contraption that looks like a four-sided cheese grater." But since I promised old Wilford I would be on my best behavior, I smiled, nodded politely, and then moved on to the next errand.

As I was crossing the street, I noticed a convoy of automobiles. There were about 30 of them, full of families and their belongings. These were the migrant workers. They were trying to escape the dust bowl. This era was full of tragedy and constant pestilence. After three years of hot weather, droughts, and over-farming of the prairie, the crops withered up and died. Rivers dried up, and wells ran dry. Many farmers at the time had a dry farming practice, relying on the rain to provide the water they needed for their crops. But now, after the disaster, the soil hardened and cracked. Then, the great winds that blew across the prairies caused dust storms. With no vegetation to stop them, the cataclysm had started. The Dust Bowl had forced a major relocation of people. I read in the papers and magazines that folk leave behind in the diner that they numbered in the millions, and this was just a tiny sample. Many towns detested these folk and had ordinances against them staying anywhere for too long.

Now, they were headed for the campgrounds. It was a smart move. They all needed to stick together and have decent access to water and sanitation. The word would get out rather quickly, and most of the townsfolk would figure out if they had any odd jobs that needed doing and would call on them. The women would go through the hand-me-down bags and bring them up to see if anyone needed anything. I knew Shelby would already be preparing boxed lunches, and they would be dropped off. We expected a large crowd of loggers and WCC workers this week, so maybe he could hire a few dishwashers. Doc Stevens, of course, would make a house call and check on everyone since the side effects of the Dust Bowl were increased death from measles, meningitis, pneumonia, and heart problems. The local farms would see if they were putting off any work or projects because they lacked the labor. This town was poor, but they would go out of their way to help those in need.

I remember last year when a group came through, a local rancher took pity on them, killed a fatted calf, and brought the cooked beast to them. They were eternally grateful. When asked why he did it, he responded, "I can't stand to see the hollow look of starvation on children's faces. It was the least that I could do. I even let them take whatever they needed from the orchards for their journey."

I quickly made my mind up and headed to the dinner. I have a spare uniform hung in the back. But I don't think I'll need it. Today, I will volunteer to help out my fellow man. When I get there, I go to the back, place the toaster on the three-compartment sink, and put on an apron.

'Dot, I can't.." Shelby started.

But I cut him off, "Shelby, I'm here to help. I'm not asking for anything. What do you need?"

"I need you to go to the storeroom and find those thick lunch boxes."

"The ones with the heavy wax?"

"That would be them."

"Isn't that a bit much for sandwiches?"

"Sandwiches? Who said anything about sandwiches? No, girl, we are going to set them up right. I counted about 30 cars, and most held at least four. So, call it 150 total. We will make them fried chicken with all the fixings."

"Shelby, we don't have the room."

"We do out back."

"Okay. But where is the chicken ?"

"I called Cuddy Farms, and they are sending them over as their contribution. Ours is to cook it and deliver it. Everyone who wants to help out is headed here. Jordan and his dad are bringing picnic tables to set up and coordinate.

The diner was situated at a crossroads and was next to a vacant lot that folks used for parking. There were a few shade trees and about a half-acre of greenery. There was a little stone wall that went around the property. Last year, the town got a grant for a beautification project, and they set the area out back into a nice, quaint little picnic area. They even put up a gazebo and a trash barrel hung on a chain. Anyone could use the picnic area, and sometimes vagrants would be outside sleeping on the benches or even curled up in the pavilion if the weather got too bad.

Two hours later, we had all the food ready and packaged. We even loaded up the picnic tables in the trucks. When we rolled in, all camp men walked forward, formed a circle, and were very wary.

I got out of Jordan's truck with a basket in my hand. I came forward and said, "Mister, we just want to help. We cooked up some fried chicken for y'all."

They were visibly relieved and waved us on up. One even said, "When y'all pulled up, we thought you were the eviction crew."

The women had tears of gratitude and accepted any help offered. Doc Stevens identified at least three women in late pregnancy and several cases of consumption. After several hours, we all returned to the diner and had coffee and bread pudding. Doc Stevens showed up and had some warm milk to go with his. "Dot, thank you for what you did today."

“Think nothing of it. I was doing what I was taught: to help your brother in his time of need.”

“Your momma would be proud.”

“Thanks.”

Shelby asked, “ So, Doc, what’s the tally?”

‘Most children have respiratory distress and a few cases of infantile paralysis.”

“What’s the treatment?”

“Fresh air for the coughing cases. I remember reading a few years back about a self-trained nurse from Queensland, Australia, who developed a therapy of moist hot packs and muscle massages with exercise. If they don’t do something soon, the muscles will atrophy, and the nerves will wither and die. Leaving permanent paralysis. They stand a good chance right now, but it will be too late if they don’t do something soon.”

“What about the pregnant women?” asked Harriet.

“We decided to move them to the Parsonage at the Baptist Church.”

“What if there are any complications?” asked Jordan's Daddy.

“Well, then we can get them over to Mt. Gilead if we have to, for the extreme cases, and New London for anything more basic.”

“All right, y’all, it’s time to lock up.”, said Shelby, “Dot, let me drive you home.”

I think of all the projects the Civilian Conservation Corps has set up throughout the area. They are determined to erect fire towers, plant over three billion trees, create state parks, and brag about employing over three million men. The tree planting is what I think is the best because before, the timber company would come in and log what they wanted and leave the rest. The forest looked like it got mugged by a bunch of drunken beavers. They would just fell everything and leave the castoffs to rot in place. In some areas, it was as barren as the moon. But now the land was to be cleared, and the forests replanted. It might take ten or twenty years, but then you would have the greenery back, and that's what I loved the best about Lake Tillery and the surrounding area. It was the trees.

"Maybe some of them folk can find work at the CCC camp in the area," I say out loud.

"I'll be sure to mention it to them. Good thinking, Dot," says Shelby.

There's No Margaritta in this Pizza

Time passes swiftly, and in the last week of school, Mrs. Maxwell comes up with a fun project again. She announces, "Today, class, we will make Margherita Pizza."

I eye the recipe card and furrow my brow. I don't have to say anything, as my face says everything.

She eyes me and says, "Yes, Dorothy-Jane, what is it?"

"Well, Mrs. Maxwell, there seems to be a mistake on the card here."

She looks perplexed and comes over to take it away and look down at it. "I don't see anything wrong."

"Well, I think a key ingredient might be missing."

"Like what?"

Then Geoff says, "Like, where is the Margarita?"

She doesn't quite understand.

And the whole class starts to twitter at the joke. Geoff mimes, pouring a pitcher into a glass and holding it to his lips. Then it dawned on her, and she chuckled. "No, no not Margarita, Margherita. Let me explain. In 1889, Raffaele Esposito invented a dish called 'Pizza Margherita' in honor of the Queen of Italy, Margherita of Savoy, and the Italian Unification. It emulated the colors of the Italian flag with red Roma tomatoes, white mozzarella, and fresh green basil. Of course, there are many variations to the story. One was that the Queen was touring Naples at the time and smelled the pizza and stopped in and requested that the owner come to the palace and cook for them. Legend has it that he did so and prepared three types of pizza, and she selected the one that would be named in honor of her as the best. All right now, let's get to work."

Geoff went to the pantry to get the ingredients, and I assembled what kitchen implements we would need. I got the rolling bin, cutting board, dough cutter, measuring cups, and thermometer. Then, we looked at the recipe cards and got to work. I assembled the flour, salt, and baking soda, and Geoff did the science part, growing the yeast. He got the water to the correct temperature and then added the yeast. We waited the appropriate amount of time and poured it into the little hole I had made at the top of the mound of flour. Then we mixed it up with our hands. I shaped it into a ball and covered it, then placed it by the warming stove and waited. While waiting for the dough to rise, we prepped the ingredients. I removed the mozzarella cheese from the container and placed it in the cheesecloth. I then wrung it out. Fresh mozzarella cheese floats in some liquid. While I was doing that, Geoff was washing the basil and tomatoes. He even found a snail sleeping on one of the leaves. He gingerly plucked it off, brought it to the potted plant on the windowsill, and placed it there. I noticed he wasn't like the other boys, all rough and tumble, snakes, snails, and puppy dog tales. No, he was more sugar and spice. Maybe I was wrong about him, and perhaps I thought he wanted to ask me out. But come to think of it, he was always chatty with the girls but had never lined one up. Maybe he had a secret and tried to share it with me, but I shot him down so abruptly and skillfully that he locked it away. Perhaps his heart wanted what it wanted as well. Maybe Geoff was hitting for the other team. I turned red with embarrassment at the realization. That boy was lonely because he could find no one that shared the same interests as him. He was the odd man out, quite literally. The realization brought tears to my eyes, and I rushed out of the classroom to get some air. I was hyperventilating and could feel one of my fits coming on. I went outside and placed my back up against the wall.

Geoff was there in a flash and could see that I was distressed and worried about myself. "Dot? You don't look so well."

"I'm sorry Geoff. I'm so very sorry.", crying uncontrollably.

"About what?" he asked in a nervous laugh.

"I'm sorry I didn't let you ask or tell me what was on your mind at the beginning of the semester. I'm sorry that, as a friend, I ignored you."

"What are you talking about?"

"About the fact that you like boys and were trying to tell me that. You just needed a friend, and I wasn't there."

"Dot there's.."

But I cut him off, "Geoff, I'm ashamed. I'm sorry, I felt overwhelmed when I realized how alone you must feel, but you don't need to comfort me; just know I'm here for you".

Now he looked scared.

"Dot. Thank you, but you can't ever.."

"Tell anyone? Yeah, I know. Because these rednecks here would lynch you for sport, they would also be very cruel about it, probably tar and feather you for good measure. I would never wish that agony on anyone. Especially not as sweet a boy as yourself."

We heard the door open, and there was Mrs. Maxwell.

"What's going on?"

"I was just checking on her," Geoff said.

I suddenly stood up, leaned over the railing, and threw up. It was very loud, and the retching continued for a bit.

"Geoff, so inside and fetch me some seltzer.", she said.

She came forward and gave me her handkerchief. I came back over the railing and gratefully accepted it. She looked at me almost heartfelt. "Dorothy-Jane, are you coming down with anything?"

"No, ma'am, I was just trying to fight off one of my fits, and this is a side effect."

"It's also a side effect if you've missed your monthly gift."

"No, ma'am, no chance of that."

"And why not? You are a decent-looking girl, healthy enough to procreate."

"The last time something like that happened, a savior was born. Ma'am, I am hermetically sealed."

"Do you need to see the school nurse?" she asked.

Just then, Geoff was back with the seltzer and a glass. She took them from him, depressed the handle, and squirted the fresh liquid, sparkling in the sunshine. She waved him away, and he returned inside. I accepted the glass, swirled it around my mouth, leaned over the railing, and spit it out.

"Could you at least be a little more ladylike?"

"Ma'am, I'm not quite sure what you mean. Do you want me to cock my left leg up while I do so?"

She tittered, "No, my dear, that would be ludicrous."

"Okay, so how, pray tell, can I be more ladylike while vomiting?"

She just sighed in exasperation and motioned for us to return inside. "If you don't feel well enough to complete the assignment, I'm sure Geoff could manage."

"Nah, he can't. I'll help him."

When the pizza dough had risen enough, we rolled it out, puncturing the bottom enough times with a fork so it could cook through and through. Then, we assembled the ingredients.

Traditional Pizza from Italy was dry. It was just tomatoes, cheese, and whatever topping you wanted. Its origin was from focaccia bread, and the wives would make it by baking the herbs and spices into the bread with tomatoes and cheese. Over time, it had morphed into what it was as it became a popular dish, and the variations started. In America, it had its origins in New York City. When the soldiers returned home from the great war, they missed the pizza they had eaten while overseas fighting. They described it to a local baker who experimented with what they told him, and American Pizza was born. It's amazing what you can pick up from the veterans. A lot of them talk about everything but the combat. They can tell you stories about the birds and what they ate, the weather, the mud, and the clouds they saw. How did the beer taste, and what did it smell like? They talked about everything important to them. Most of them came back from the Great War shattered. So, they stopped remembering what to do and focused on everything else to keep sane.

I looked down at what I considered a pretty shabby piece of work. No, it seemed all right, but I could tell that it would also be very disappointing. We doused it in olive oil and then threw it into the oven to bake. We even had a little dough left over, so Geoff and I thrashed the tomatoes and smeared them onto the dough. Geoff had secretly found some pepperoni in the pantry, and we furtively sliced it up and added it to the pizza. Then, put it in the oven in the smaller pan.

While waiting, I asked Geoff, “How do you know about Margaritas?”

“Oh, my family and I were on vacation in Texas, and they were all the rage. Every place sells them, and they taste pretty good.”

“What about prohibition?”

“We were in a border town called Juarez. It doesn’t apply there.”

“It’s just lime juice, crushed ice, and tequila, right?”

“Yes, with salt around the rim. But they also make them in Mango and Strawberry.”

“Sounds pretty good. But I don’t drink.”

“Maybe I could make some up for you sometime.”

“Check with Mrs. Maxwell. Maybe we can incorporate that into a future class assignment.”

“Sounds like a plan.” he said as he went over to the ‘idea jar’ and got a slip of paper.

He returned and asked, “What would be the best way to describe I want to serve mixed drinks in class?”

‘As a hostess, what are the best choices for libations to entertain at a cocktail party?’ Then, suggest the strawberry margarita. See if she bites. What’s the worst that could happen? She says no?”

We chuckled at that.

The next thing we knew, it was time to remove the pizzas from the oven. We pulled them out and saw that the beautiful leaves had shriveled from the oven's heat.

"Now, class, let the pizzas rest for about a minute or two. Then, cut them up. We will use the party cut since we need so many pieces for each class member to try." She motioned to the board, and we saw she had put a grid up.

"You would remove it from the pan by sliding it onto the cutting board and then chop it in half vertically. Then, in half equally and again, proceed to cut horizontally. When you are done, there should be twenty-two pieces."

She went down the rows and graded each one on appearance. She then tasted each one as well.

"Charlotte, yours has the right look, but something is off in the taste; I think you used too much salt."

"Mabel. Yours was raw at the bottom. You must remember to puncture the crust enough so that the moisture can escape."

"Geoff, yours was fine, but why did you make two?"

"We had extra dough left over and decided to waste not."

She reached over and picked up a piece, evening it carefully. "I see you made a variation with pepperoni. Not on the assignment," she said; she popped it into her mouth and then scrawled it across her sheet. Then, he smiled and continued.

"Charlotte, the pizza crust is supposed to be thick and chewy, while yours is hard and crumbly. Any thoughts?"

"No, ma'am. It's my first time.", she said, looking worried.

Mrs. Maxwell turned around and addressed us all. "Class, today's exercise is only graded on class participation. Don't look so worried. All of your grades stand."

I saw Mabel sobbing in a corner, so I looked at Geoff, who nodded.

I asked Mabel, "Honey, what's wrong?"

She was a petite girl of four foot eleven with green eyes and curly brown locks. She always dressed conservatively and was very prim and proper, just mousy.

“I’ll never get any of this right. I’m an utter failure.”

“Mabel, we are all learning. That’s the point of the class.”

“I’ll never find a husband.”

“What makes you say that?”

“Well, just look at me.”

“You look fine.”

“No, I don’t. I’m short and fat.”

“Now stop that, you hear,” I said rather sharply. “You are a beautiful girl. You are petite.”

“But I’m fat.”

“No, you are stout. It’s just the way god made you. You are built for comfort, not speed.”

She gave a peculiar look. So, I explained. “Men are attracted to a certain type of woman. They want a woman who can give them children and have enough fat to survive the winter. That is what breasts are: fat reserves. They give milk, of course. But it's ingrained into their minds. Now, boys are another matter. But men know the worth of a woman. They want a study woman to be able to handle a farm and the rigors and hardships that go with it. We are there to support each other. The men hunt, and the women gather, cook, clean, and watch the children. I think you are just shopping in the wrong area. Maybe you need to find someone who will appreciate you as you are. Possibly some professor type.”

“But look at you, you are perfect.”

“Perfect? Mabel, my measurements are 15, 15, 15. I’m built like a 15-year-old boy. I have absolutely no breasts. I’m a carpenter's dream.”

“What does that mean?”

“That I’m flat as a board and never been nailed.”

She chortled at that.

Mrs. Maxwell coughed slightly behind us. “Everything all right?”

“Yes, Ma’am, just girl talk.”, I said.

She promptly left.

Mabel said again, “But all the boys talk to you.”

“Them boys are scared of me. Have been since I put the fear of god into them in first grade. I’m not sure if you notice, but the ones that talk to me more than once do it on a dare.”

“Really?”

“Yep, that’s the first prank for anyone new in town. ‘Go talk to the crazy girl.’

“I never knew that.”, she said, then she set her face. “That’s mean.”

“Yeah, but boys will be boys. No real harm in talking.”

“But you deserve better.”

“I have better.”

“Who?”

“Actually, it's whom.”

“Okay, then, whom?”

“Delbert.”

“Delbert?”

"Yes, Delbert."

"Okay, I get it; y'all have been friends since childhood. But don't you want something else?"

"Nope. We are soul mates. Have been ever since we met. We're both a little broken; hence, we need each other."

"Delbert. Okay. I guess you would know best."

Schools Out Forever

Time passes, and school is out forever. Delbert and me done graduated. Everyone in the town took up a collection that they called my college fund. But they knew I was never going there.

The Mayor, old Joe, came into the diner one day, beaming with pride. He said, “May I have your attention, everyone.”

The diner fell silent. He could be such a ham sometimes. He continued, “Dot, get on over here.”

I walked forward to the register. He held out his hand, and in it was a rather large facsimile of a check.

“I would like to present this check here on behalf of the entire town of Lake Tillery and the village of Misenheimer. These funds are your graduation present. Now, you can use it any way that you wish.”

“Like what?” I asked playfully.

“Like college, secretarial or beauty school and things like that.”

“Why, thank you all. I will take this check and get it deposited right away.” I knew I was playing to the crowd as I saw the newspaper reporter from New London.

Every business and just about everyone had contributed to this. I would have to find some enterprising way to use the funds that would not disappoint them. I already had the germ of an idea. I just needed to get a few of the particulars together.

What I wanted to do was to buy and stock a cigarette machine. I realized I would have to make my money back from the initial investment, but I didn't think it would be far off the way everyone smoked like chimneys. Since the tobacco was grown locally in Winston-Salem, it should be cheaper to set up everything.

I asked Shelby if I could, and he said yes. He even made the call to Winston-Salem and ordered one. He hung up and said, "Dot, they will be here on Wednesday. Then, we will sit down and discuss the particulars.

Wednesday rolled around, and the salesman, Mr. Lowenstein, arrived at 5:30 in the morning and explained,

" The way it works is we own the machine and are responsible for stocking and maintaining it. We will come by once a month to count out the cash box and split everything 50/50. Call it in if you run out of at least half of the inventory, and we will come running since we have men out on the route and can have someone as early as the next day."

"Or?"

"Or you can buy and stock the machine yourself. Then all maintenance is on you. The cost per pack will be higher. If it gets broken or vandalized, you must order parts, etc."

"Okay, I get it. I'm probably better off with the first option."

"Good girl. You are at least 18 and can sign a contract, correct?"

"Yes, sir, and according to this, I can also set the price on the machine by, at most, a nickel higher if I so choose?"

"You may?"

"And if I do, then I can keep any overage, and that's not part of the split."

Yes?"

"Great. Then what is the suggested retail price?"

"Fifteen cents."

"All right. Then, I would like to set the price at 20 cents."

"Any particular reason?"

"Yes. This place is a crossroads, and we have a lot of people that pass through, and some of them are used to higher prices. Plus, stocking dimes is a lot easier than stocking twice as many nickels."

"Wow. Shelby, she's a smart one."

"Little miss?"

"Dorothy Jane."

"Sorry, Miss Dorothy."

"It's Dorothy-Jane. Please pronounce my whole name since my mother took the time to give it to me."

He smiled pensively and started again," All right, Miss Dorothy-Jane. How much product do you expect to need? The machine holds 12 different brands. And we will even throw in this little slot machine. For a penny, people can try to line up three of a kind, and they will receive a token good for one pack of cigarettes. You will have the key and can keep all of those profits. We will deduct any tokens from the split. Is that acceptable?"

"I dunno, Shelby? What do you think?"

"Well, we can try out one and see what happens."

Mr. Lowenstein nodded to the route manager, who set up the slot machine by the register. Then we resumed talking. "We have

Camels, Chesterfields, Lucky Strike, Pall Mall for our military folks. Chelsea, Domino, and Craven "A" Virginia Cigarettes for the ladies. Winston, Salem, North State, Marlboro, and Benson & Hedges for everyone else."

"Sir, I don't smoke, so how will I be able to describe the differences?"

"I have some sample pamphlets for you. Also, we have a smaller vending machine that we can place on a wall by the phone booth if you wish. The cost for those is a nickel, and it only dispenses three cigarettes in a pack. Only two brands are available because of its size, but it comes with matches. We can rotate what's available over time. We will give you a few sample cartons of cigarettes and two cases of matches, one hard and one soft. They are a penny each, your cost. You can sell them or give them away. Most vendors use the income from the slot machine to pay for the matches. If you sell over 20 cartons of cigarettes a month, you will get two free cases of matches of your choice. We will also provide any advertising posters or table tents as you wish. From time to time, we will run promotions and will let you know in advance what they are. Do you have any questions?"

" It all seems rather straightforward, but in the event of an odd number of sales, in whose favor does the odd one go to?"

"That would be you since you have the real estate."

"So, all in all, we are getting three vending machines for the price of one?"

"Essentially."

"The main cigarette machine has a 50/50 split, but we keep the extra nickel?"

"Yes."

"Then we keep all sales from the slot machine, but with the caveat that any tokens redeemed would come out of our split on the main machine?"

"Yes."

"How would that work?"

"Well, when it comes time to count. The tokens would be counted first. Then, one dime would be removed for each. We would compare the number of packs sold and remove one dime for each. The remainder would be yours. It's a much cleaner way of counting with your proposal. Because before, it was a split of 7.5 cents per pack sold."

"Okay, I think I got it. So, the smaller machine by the phone only gives three cigarettes and free matches for a nickel. But there are only two brands available on a rotational basis."

"Yes."

"So, if someone spent twenty cents on that machine, they would end up with two free cigarettes and free matches."

"Yes. But it was set up based on fifteen cents a pack of ten, so originally, they would end up with nine cigarettes and free matches. It still works out great for the customer because now they can buy a sample pack if they are unsure, and everyone wins."

"Okay. I understand. Just one more question? What is the total yield?"

"Each slot holds 25 packs, and there are 14 brands so that the total would be 350 packs for the main machine. Therefore, the total sales price should be around $70. Minus the split and any free packs, you should expect the monthly income to be in the $20-30 range."

"And I just need to sign here?"

“Yes.”

So, I signed and wondered how long it would take to make real money. I didn’t have to wait too long because of all the public works projects. There was a steady flow of truckers and timber workers coming through. I let Shelby keep the free samples. I just took one packet of each for reference. We had to call for them to swing by and empty the coins three days later. They were impressed. I offered to let Shelby keep the income from the smaller machine at the phone booth, but he was having none of it. He said, “No, girl. This is your idea. You came up with it and ran with it. This will make you money while you are away at school, off work, or on vacation. You have three extra streams of income. Well done.”

“But don’t I owe you rent for the machines?” I asked.

“No. Because now we have free advertising for the diner, which draws more people in. As Mr. Lowenstein said. Everybody wins.”

“I hung a clipboard in the back to track the sales. “

“Good thinking.”

One day, I got a package in the mail. When I opened it up, it was four little vending machines about three- and three-quarter inches high by six and a half inches wide. It was a chrome bank designed to hold only twenty cigarettes. And you put a penny in, and it dispensed one. Cute.

That first month, after expenses, I made $100 from the sale of cigarettes and $15 from the slot machine. It was remarkable. Here I was, a girl with barely $3 to her name, and now had multiple income streams. I was making money while I slept.

****

Stumbling Around

One day in June, I woke up and was feeling poorly. I couldn't concentrate. I knew it wasn't related to my womanly schedule. I felt like there was some buzzing in my head that wouldn't quit. I tried to shake it off, but it was right there. I was almost late for my shift. When I entered, Shelby looked at me and motioned me to go out back. I did, and his face was real stern.

"What is it, Shelby?" I asked pensively.

"Dot! Are you coming down with something?"

"Not that I know of why?"

"Because your face is grey, and your lips are blue. You know that we can't have you sick working around food. I'll call you a cab. You can come back when you feel better."

"Sure," I said. Then suddenly, I jerked and fell out. I found out what happened afterward.

Shelby had turned away, but he heard me crash into the cans. He yelled, "Jesus Christ! HARRIET!!!"

She stuck her head out and said, "WHAT?"

"Call an ambulance. Dot done fell out."

"Is she shaking and having one of her fits?"

"Nope. She's out cold. Hurry up, girl. Ambulance!"

They called, and it turned out it would take about two hours to get one. Someone called the Doc, and Jordan Belfry offered to drive us to Troy. I was in and out of it. My teeth were chattering, and I was cold all over. They laid me in the back of the truck bed and put a Woolrich Blanket over me. It was one of the fancy types that wealthy people used to decorate their sofas. It was rich and warm. Doc Stevens was concerned. When they got me to Troy and pulled in, the receiving crew took one look at me and started backing away. They turned and ran back inside, yelling, "CODE BLACK! Get all safety and quarantine gear now!" They had locked the door. Doc and Jordan were perplexed. About three minutes later, the team exited the front door and surrounded Doc and Jordan.

"Whom has been in direct contact with the girl?" asked the lead Physician.

"Me.", answered Doc.

"Whom else?"

"Shelby and Harriet"

"Where are they?"

"Back at Lake Tillery running the diner."

"Dear GOD. Send the recovery team there. Quarantine them if need be. Shut that diner down if necessary."

"You?" they asked Jordan.

He just shook his head. "I just drove."

"Fine. Step to the right."

He did, and the team started to examine him on the spot. After a few minutes, they nodded and had him come inside for observation. They would end up releasing him a few hours later.

The double doors burst open, and they rolled out a large piece of metal equipment that looked like a larger version of a 55-gallon oil drum. They opened it up and placed me inside. Only my head was visible. The crown was made of plexiglass. They put a mask on me and covered my head with a paper cap. They rolled me inside, and Doc Stevens followed.

They cut my clothes off of my body and were instructed to burn it all. They even torched the blanket. Doc Stevens had no idea why they were reacting the way they did. But he found out in short order.

The lead physician was called Wolfgang Mueller. He told Doc, "Sorry if our methods seem to be a bit extreme, but that girl has all the signs of tuberculosis."

"Why the code black?"

"Has she ever been out of the country?"

"Hardly ever out of the county. One thing, she does have epilepsy."

"When was her last episode?"

"A few months back, when she found out her momma died."

"The shock of that type of news could cause anyone to react that way. Has she recently had any Grand Mal Seizures?"

"Not in a long time. What else is worrying you?"

"We did a spinal tap on her, and she is also showing symptoms of Spinal meningitis."

"So, she has both a viral and bacteriological infection?"

"I know it sounds bizarre as they should be mutually exclusive; however, we are trying to save her life, which will be the best way to treat her. We are trying to avoid septicemia. At least you got her here in time, so I don't think there will be any damage to the brain or nerves. But now she has a trifecta going on.

“That’s going to be some paper that you publish in JAMMA. If you don’t mind my asking, where did you receive your training?”

“The Julius- Maximilian’s..”

“Universität Wurzburg,” Doc Stevens finished for him.

“You know of the place?”

“I’d heard about it at a conference in Dusseldorf.”

“The one that took place when the Great War broke out?”

“The same. Did you serve?”

He swallowed hard and said, “I’ll just table that for now.”

Changing subjects, Doc Stevens said, “So that school seems to specialize in the detection and treatment of infectious diseases diagnosis and tropical medicine. It’s good that you were on staff when we brought her here. What did I miss?”

“Sir, you didn’t miss anything. It was just that the condition that she was brought in triggered a memory from when I was serving in Burma. Many locals came down with tuberculosis, and cholera was rampant. Her legs had red, angry, hard splotches. Calling the Code Black was imperative if she was infectious. Plus, it triggers more safety features for the staff and patients on hand.”

“I’m not questioning your judgment since your training is ideal for the patient I brought in. Just curious. Why the Iron Lung?”

“It was thc bcst way to isolate her as it sealed her inside completely as the units on hand had a plexiglass cap. You are free to go. Sorry for the scare. But we had to take every precaution.”

“Where is she?”

“We’ve wheeled her down to the best place for extreme isolation.”

“The morgue?”

“Yes. That girl is fighting for her life, but she is so skinny. I wonder if she will make it?”

“That girl is too ornery to die. She came out of the womb full of piss and vinegar. I’m not leaving. But I must tell Jordan to return to Lake Tillery without me.”

“He’s already gone. We can set you up in the overnight doctor's suite.”

“That would be very kind of you. Thanks”

The Looney Bin

The next several days went by in a flash. I remember waking up really thirsty, a straw being held to my lips, and the crisp taste of apple juice running down my raw throat. I couldn't focus on anything. My vision was blurry, and everyone's voices sounded like they were talking underwater. I had been poked and prodded and felt deep stabbing pains in my left hip. Also, my back was very sore, and I felt a pinching all over.

It turns out that they were taking my spinal fluid daily. The way that they do this is to take a rather large hollow needle and puncture the lower lumbar. The device has a handgrip, and they spin a screw to tighten it. Then, they draw the spinal fluid and test it. Next, they remove it, add some medicine, and insert it back into the spine. The whole thing is made of shiny stainless steel. It doesn't hurt, but the side effect is a painful headache. But I was so out of it that I couldn't tell the difference.

Sometime later, I awoke in a new facility. They told me I had been transferred to the only place with the required long-term quarantine facilities. I was shipped to Morganton to the Western North Carolina Insane Asylum. It was built in 1878 and has a Colonial Revival Art Deco style. It sat on a 283-acre plot of land, and they had their farm, a dairy, a vineyard, and greenhouses. Patients of varying degrees of lucidity ran all of these. It was, for the most part, self-sufficient. There was just one major problem. The irony was not lost on me.

My whole life, people had called me "That Crazy girl." And here I am in the only place with the proper facilities to care for me, which turns out to be the 'Looney Bin.' How in the hell am I ever going to get out of here?

I prop myself up and take a hard look around. Here, I am in a hospital ward. There are twenty-five beds on each wall, with a middle area with the same number. So, each ward houses up to 75 patients, all in varying degrees of functionality. Two desks were on each end of the ward—one for each Registered Nurse. There were many support staff on hand, like orderlies and nursing trainees. I also see a small trunk at the end of the beds. There is also a nightstand that has a Bible and a water glass. As I try to get out of bed, a small girl of about 15 stops me. She put her hand on my chest and said, "Take it easy. You've been here for over a month."

"Is that why everything hurts and my mouth tastes like metal?"

"Yes. Let me see about getting you some wheels."

"What?" I ask.

"I'll be right back with a wheelchair, as you aren't going to make it out of the ward.", she said. She's charming with a pixie haircut. Of course, we are all dressed alike in a nightgown and a blue robe with slippers. As I sat on the edge of the bed, trying not to get vertigo, she returned with the wheelchair.

"Are you strong enough to do this?" I ask.

"Nope, but you are. Just turn the wheels, and I'll steer."

"What's your name?"

"Kylen"

"That's a nice one. Irish?"

"As Irish as they come."

"Where are we off to?"

"Where did you want to go?"

"The bathroom."

"Why?"

"I really need to pee. Then a bath."

"We can't take baths here. Only showers. If we require a bath, it must be approved by a doctor and then supervised by a nurse. But I wouldn't suggest it."

"Why not?"

"Because they don't like to be bothered, and they will use a horsehair brush on you and scrape a few layers of skin off you just to prove a point."

"That being?"

"That they don't like to do it. Don't want to do it and don't want you asking for it ever again."

She steered us down the hall to the toilets. There were no stalls for privacy. Everything was out in the open. I was too tired to care. So, I did my business and felt tender down there. She could see my discomfort and told me, "They had a catheter on you. That's why it feels strange and stings."

"Makes sense if I've been mostly comatose. Next stop." I said as I dropped into the chair. She spun me around, and we headed to the quartermasters to get my supplies. I was issued one bar of soap, a toothbrush, a tin cup, a towel, feminine napkins, washcloths, and a small canvas bag to lug around. The attendant asked me for my patient number, and I just shrugged.

"She's 23."

"How do you know?"

"It's on the wall above your bed, silly."

"Good to know."

He gave me a small metal token and showed me how to tie it to my bag. He also gave me one on a string I had to wear around my neck. This was to identify me as an outpatient here for quarantine medical purposes. "Don't lose this, or you will get lost in the shuffle and never leave here."

"Thank you, sir. " I said sweetly as he headed off to the next stop. "Where to next?"

"The showers."

So, we went down the hallway that looked identical to the others. How she could tell her way around this place was lost to me, but I guess I would get used to it. She wheeled us to the showers, and I disrobed, sat on a chair, and let the water wash over me. She stayed back a respectful distance and took her shower. She was very modest, and I noticed that there was a scar along her side that was shaped like a fishbone. Once she was finished, she shut off the water when I nodded to her. She helped me rise and towel off. Then, he helped me get dressed and dry my hair a bit. I saw a comb and bush in the kit I had missed earlier.

"What's next?"

"Well, we're close enough to the cafeteria, and since it's almost that time, we can grab some lunch."

"Steer away."

We went down the hall and came across a rather large meeting room marked Cafetorium. I wrinkled my face up on that one, and she giggled.

“Did someone smoke reefer when they were painting that sign?” I asked in all seriousness.

“Nah. It’s just a made-up name for a multi-use area. It’s mostly used as a cafeteria but can also be used as an auditorium.”

We lined up, and some sandwiches were wrapped in wax paper. They were cut in a triangle and double stacked, then wrapped on each end. She piled the food onto the tray and clipped onto my chair at the armrest. She grabbed two pieces of fruit, an apple and a pear. Then she picked up two chubs of milk and two small salad bowls. A spoon was all we had to eat anything with, and it was lousy for salad. We rolled over to the table by the window at the far end of the hall. I could feel the warmth of sunshine on my face.

“Which sandwich do you want?” she asked.

“Don’t care. Get whatever you want.”, I told her.

“Okay. I like peanut butter, so I’ll get this one and the pear. The other one is tuna fish that pairs well with apple.” She snorted in laughter at the double entendre.

I groaned.

We ate the meal, mostly in silence. I could see that she wanted to talk and needed a friend. But I was too distracted to notice.

After a time, she meekly asked me, “Dorothy-Jane?”

“Yes?”

“Did I do anything wrong?”

“No. Why do you ask?”

“Because you are not talking.”

“Oh, sorry. I am still getting used to being here, and the whole thing is a big change from where I was, and I’m just tired.”

"Right. Let's get you back."

We returned to the ward, and she rolled me right up to the bed, where I flopped.

"Good night.", she said sweetly.

"Night." I groaned even though it was barely noon.

Eyes in the Night

I awoke sometime in the night to hear a patient moaning. I propped myself up to see medical staff hurrying to the bed opposite mine on the far wall. They grabbed the privacy curtain and closed it around themselves. But because of the night lighting setup, they were perfectly illuminated. So, it was pointless to try to obscure what they were doing. I looked to my left and saw Kylen staring at them and huddled in absolute fear. I tossed back the covers and motioned for her to come over, and she jumped. She hopped into my bed and hugged me tight. I didn't know what upset her, so I just went with it—making shushing noises and distracting her from the unfolding episode. The next thing I knew, I awoke to her snuggling up next to me, and we held hands. Boy, my neck sure did hurt. I looked up to see a nurse looking at my chart. She looked at me and sternly said, "23, why are you and 18 in bed together?"

"She got scared."

"There were no weather events last night. So, I ask again."

"She got scared at what was happening over there," I said as I pointed at the empty bed.

"I see. Well, we have rules around here.", she began.

"Ma'am, I just woke up from a coma. I'll be happy for you to read me the riot act once I have been apprised of 'The Rules'. Would you like to recite them, or do you give a pamphlet or contract written in legalize, bathed in medical terminology, wrapped inside an enigma, sprinkled with Latin, and hidden in a conundrum?"

"Noted. You have a spinal tap this morning. Get in the chair.", she said rather crisply. But I also saw a sly nod of appreciation. I know that I have a mouth on me. I have always had. But as I got older, I was finding ways to be clever versus just 'beating them over the head with the truth,' as my momma would call it.

I complied, and an orderly steered me toward the procedure room. I was given a hospital gown and allowed to change behind a privacy screen. I didn't care, but they had their 'Rules'. So, I obliged. They helped me up to the exam table, a stainless-steel contraption with drains on each side. It gave me the creeps as it looked like it belonged in a morgue. I lay on my stomach, and a nurse's assistant held my hands straight. Another had my feet. I was told to keep my chin up until they were done. I couldn't feel it, but I started sweating after a few minutes in this uncomfortable position. Then they declared, "Done," and I was released from what I called the 'drawn and quartered position.' Of course, I didn't tell them that, lest they think I was addled and needed to stay. I was told to remain still for a few minutes, and then they rolled me over and into the chair. My nightgown was placed in the seat back, and I was rolled to breakfast. Once there, the staff was instructed to provide me with a fried egg and rice bowl. I was also given apple juice. When I asked if I could have coffee, they recoiled at the thought.

"Why on earth would you want stimulants?"

"So, iced tea is also out of the question?"

The frown deepened.

"Okay. No dice. Wonderful. That will only add to the massive headache I feel coming on."

A cart with little paper cups was wheeled over, and I was given two pills and a glass of water.

"What are these?"

"Why does it matter?" asked the girl running the cart.

"Well, I am not on any medication I know of, so…."

"It's just aspirin, dear.", she said, slightly miffed.

"Great. Thanks."

I was wheeled to the Day Room and left alone in the chair. I heard music playing, so I wheeled to the Gramophone. It was playing "Blue Moon". I closed my eyes and just listened to the lyrics. Richard Rodgers could write a ballad, but he didn't do it alone, as he had help from Lorentz Hart. Connee Boswell sang the song, and she was one of 'The Boswell Sisters'. She was born in Kansas City but raised in New Orleans, and you could tell by her rich Southern accent. I remember hearing her perform live on the radio from the Orpheum Theater in New Orleans. She was singing 'Crying Blues,' I swear I thought it was Mamie Smith. How do I know all of this? Because I read the trades that people left behind at the diner.

I hear my name called excitedly, and Kylen runs over and hugs me. I can feel she's shaking.

"What's up, buttercup?" I ask with genuine concern.

"Why did you disappear? I thought you died."

"No, dear, I just had to have a spinal tap. I'll have one every morning. So, if you don't see me, that's where I'm at." This girl has some issues, but I can hardly blame her.

After a time, the nurses came in and told us it was time to leave the day room to make way for the next group. Kylen told me, "We are only allowed an hour in there each day. But the grounds are free, so let's roam.", she said excitedly.

So, roam, we did. The place had some lovely gardens, and I could see honeybees dancing in flight as they went from flower to flower, collecting pollen. And I could see hummingbirds doing the same, but they were eating the nectar from the flowers and humming their tune. I could see a honeysuckle growing up the side of a pergola, so I asked Kaylen, "Can you steer me over there to the honeysuckle?"

"Sure, why?"

"Have you never had some?"

"Somewhat?"

"Honeysuckle."

"I'm not sure what you mean."

I grinned, "Then you are in for a treat." I said as I reached up and gently plucked a flower and held it out to her. She took it and was puzzled.

"Go on."

"Go on what?"

"Lift it to your lips and lean back."

She did, and I could see the amazement on her face. "Wow", she said, "That's magical."

"You don't get out much, do you?"

"No. I worked at a Greensboro factory and came down with tuberculosis. That's why I ended up here."

"Any family?"

"My aunt, Siobhan."

“Does she visit?”

“She can’t, as we are in quarantine. But she writes letters and occasionally sends treats, like Irish shortbread biscuits.”

We sat there, and I started to get hot. She noticed the sweat on my brow; she grinned and said. “Hey there, now let me show you something.”, she said as she went over to the fountain and grabbed a small ladle. She dipped it into the water and poured it over the honeysuckle. The wind blew, and I felt cool air blowing over my skin.

“That’s just luverly.”, I said, intentionally mispronouncing the word playfully.

“Neato.”

We noticed a grey tabby cat walk by with a kitten in its mouth. Kylen cooed, “Oh, a kitten.”

We saw that she was headed over to the kitchen's back door. We followed her and saw that a small apple crate had been set up with a blanket, water, and food. The momma cat plopped down and started to bathe the runaway, and the other kittens were mewling as they sought a nipple and got to work feeding.

“Don’t go disturbing anything, girl,” said a baritone voice. I looked up to see a massive man looming over us. His skin was dark as midnight. It was so black that it had a blue tinge to it. He was dressed as a cook with white chef's pants and a jacket, which was unbuttoned and showed off his wife's beater t-shirt underneath. “Who’s your friend?”

“That’s Dorothy-Jane.”

“My friends call me Dot,” I said, smiling at him. All I could see was kindness.

"Oh, sorry, I didn't know."

"That's fine, dear. I've been out of it."

"Well, Dot. This here is Charlton."

He reached over and shook my hand. His paws were like a grizzly bear, reminding me of Delbert. So much that it made me tear up. He noticed my discomfort and asked, "What's wrong?"

"Nothing. You remind me of my soul mate, Delbert."

"Has he passed on?" he asked.

"No. I'm just trapped here for god knows how long, and I've been awake for two days and have not seen a doctor or apprised of my condition. All I know is that they keep giving me a spinal tap and put medicine in the fluid."

"Oh… you that one."

"That one what?"

"The girl who shouldn't be alive. The one with two conditions that shouldn't intermingle was destined to die. He was being deemed too skinny to survive. You've been in a coma for over a month. I'm glad you made it.", he said, smiling. "Peanut?" he asked as he produced one from his pocket.

I leaned forward and took it from his hand, which was as large as a ham. That's when I noticed the tattoo on his arm. "You're a Harlem Hell fighter?"

It was his turn to look uncomfortable. "What do you know about that?" he asked a little sourly.

Kylen looked perplexed. So, I informed her that "Charlton here was a member of the 369th Infantry Regiment; they started as the 15th New York National Guard Regiment before being consolidated into the 369th. They fought in France and were a very courageous bunch.

So much so that 171 members were awarded the Croix de Guerre medal and a unit citation for everyone else; that's Frances's version of the Medal of Honor. This man here is a hero through and through. It's an honor to meet you."

"How can a white girl like you know about a colored regiment in the Great War?"

"Well, a lot of the men in my community, Lake Tillery, served in France, and the exploits of your regiment are legendary. My Godfather, Sherriff Wilford Funderburk, always tells stories of your men's courage, dedication, and service."

"Serving in the military is not all glory. It's painful, hard work."

"Sir, while you were fighting my family, everyone else got to sleep safely through the night. Because you were at your post, fighting them over there, so we didn't have to fight them over here. I am and will always be grateful to any military man, no matter the length of their service."

He nodded in agreement and left it at that. He stood up and said, "I'll be right back." A few minutes later, he returned with a small, chipped plate with a few sardines. "Here you go. You can feed her while she feeds them."

So we did, and he smiled at us. Just a couple of kids being entertained by a mother cat and her kittens. Then, once the job was completed, he said, "Y'all get back now." As he snuffed out his cigarette and returned to the kitchen.

We returned to the ward, and I was mad at myself for being too weak. So, I asked Kylen if there was a gym.

"Yes, but we only get to go there on Wednesdays."

"Fine. What day is today?"

"Tuesday."

"All right. You mentioned getting letters from your aunt. Since I've been here for over a month, how would I check if I have any letters?"

"Just ask one of the Nurses."

"Okay. I think I will." So, I wheeled myself over to the head Nurse. Hildegard. When I arrived, she didn't even look up from the mountain of paperwork and charts covering her desk.

"Yes?" she asked in a bored tone.

"Ma'am, I was just wondering if I have received any correspondence?"

"Number?"

"23?"

"Is that a question or a statement?"

"It's a statement."

"Let's see.", she said as she opened a drawer, and I saw that many letters within were wrapped up in different colored ribbons. "Ah, yes. Here you are.", she said as she handed me a packet of correspondence. She never once looked me in the eye. To her, I was just a number. I didn't even deserve a name.

"Thanks.", I said meekly as I laid the letters in my lap, turned the wheelchair around, and returned to bed. Once there, I opened them up and placed them in chronological order based on the Postmark days.

"Kylen, is there a library around here?"

"Of course. Let's go.", she said as she hopped up and wheeled me to wherever it was. On the way, I asked her," How do you know where to go?"

“What do you mean?” she asked.

“All of the corridors look the same.”

“Oh, that. Well, you get used to it.”, she said as she shrugged. We turned a corner, and there we were. I could have sworn this was the way to the Cafetorium, but the door sign said Library. We entered, and there were books everywhere. Stacks and stacks of them. All are neatly aligned, and everything is in its place. We went over to a table, and I laid out all the letters and started reading. She went to the periodicals and returned with a small stack of Look Magazine, Hush, Hush, and the like. She motioned for me to continue, and so I did.

The first letter was from Doc Stevens,

Dot,

I’m sorry we had to send you to that place, but we were trying to save your life. You have three separate conditions that should be mutually exclusive, but they are all running concurrently. Since they slapped you inside that Iron Lung, we are all worried about you. Rest up, dear, and I pray that you get better. …….

With Love,

Richard Stevens, M.D.

She asked Kylen, “What does concurrently mean?”

“It means at the same time.”

“And Mutually exclusive?”

“I dunno. I guess we ask a grownup.”

“Or I could look it up in the dictionary.”

“That’s a thought,” Kylen said as she got up, went to the reference books section, and returned with one. She furrowed her brow and just read, “It’s a statistical term describing two or more events that cannot happen simultaneously. For example, War and Peace cannot exist simultaneously.”

The next one was from Shelby,

Dot,

We felt scared. I hope you come out on the other side of this. A-ok. The last time I was fearful for another’s life was during the Great War. We received a notice from the Red Cross that my brother Tim was listed as missing in action. I was worried sick as I was serving as a cook on a Destroyer; knowing he was missing and unable to do anything about it made me sick, just like when you fell out. Please don’t scare me like that again. Get well, and we’ll see you soon.

With much love

Shelby

The following letter was from Sheriff Funderburk

Dot,

I’m sorry that we missed you being sick. We feel bad that we weren’t aware you were so bad off. You gave the whole town quite a scare. They sent a team from Troy to check out everyone, but only Harriet and Shelby had contact with you. They have no idea where it came from or how it got to you. I know where we ended up placing you was not ideal, but it was necessary as you were at death's door. The long-term care and rehabilitation have to happen there. Get better and gather your strength. We’ll be seeing you soon. Old

Wilford (Don't think I don't know that's what you call me behind my back)

You always make me smile, dear.

Then, the most heartbreaking was a postcard from Delbert.

Dot,

Please don't leave me. Come back. My momma is gone now, just like yours.

Come back to me

With all my love

Delbert

The last letter was from Anthony.

Dear Dorothy-Jane,

I miss having you around. I behave well at the Sheriff's house and am always on my best behavior, saying yes sir and no ma'am and please and thank you. I don't even ask for dessert.

Please get well and come home.

Love

Anthony

Sitting there, I swore to do whatever was required to return home to Lake Tillery. I had to return to the people who cared for and loved me. They stood behind me even when I knew I was on their last nerve. Because to them, I was family. They might not be related by blood, but that wasn't always necessary. I will ensure that when I return, I will thank all of them.

I noticed a newspaper was in her stack of periodicals, and on the front page was a story about New Orleans City Park getting expanded by the CCC Projects. They built sidewalks, bridges, and an art museum. So, the economy and progress were chugging along. I then sought out the recipe section. I sifted through the duds like a game meat pie. 'Sorry, not that desperate'. Here's a real winner: Pigeon and Mushroom Stew: three pigeons, fat, gravy or stock, cream, mushrooms, cayenne, salt, pepper, and mushroom catsup. I could manage that. Then, another one caught my eye: Creole Sauce: Chopped onion, minced green peppers, butter, flour, salt and pepper, tomatoes, bouillon, and sliced mushrooms. Once I get out of here, I think I'll make these. Or maybe I can get Charlton to try these out in the kitchen.

Sensing I was done, Kylen put away her magazines, and we left the Library.

As we turned down an older corridor, I asked her, "Where are we going?"

"Oh, I've just got to make a small stop, as I need something."

"So, are we going to the hospital store?"

"Something like that.", Kaylen answered mysteriously.

We stopped at a broom closet, and she rapped three times. A figure slid a note underneath, and she scooped it up. She looked down at it, smiled, then nodded, and we resumed the journey.

"Okay, Kylen, that was weird. What are we doing?"

"I've got to get some cigarettes."

"Cigarettes?"

"Aren't you a bit young for that?"

"I'm old enough to work, then I'm old enough to smoke."

"Listen, I've got cigarettes back in my trunk."

"Sure, you do.", she said slowly and sarcastically. "Dot, you don't smoke. I can smell the tobacco on people who smoke."

"Kylen, back home, I'm a waitress in a diner in Lake Tillery, and I am a half-partner in two cigarette vending machines and a slot machine. I can give you a pack."

"A whole pack?'

"Yes. Let's turn around and get out of here. This doesn't feel right."

"What kind?"

"I don't know," I said, thinking real hard as to which one I had in my purse at the time, "Craven "A" Virginia Cigarettes."

"Craven "A"? Sorry, never heard of them.", she said as she continued to steer us down the hall.

My mind was racing, "How about Domino? It's all the rage."

She stopped pushing for half a tic, looked down at me, and said mockingly, "Dot, I think you are telling a fib. Oh, well. Too late. We are here." She said as she pulled up to a meeting room and rapped her knuckles lightly. The door very slowly opened. She pushed us inside, and everything was in shadow. This made my nerves go on edge, and I was on the verge of panic and could feel a fit coming on. I gasped and said, "Kylen, what's the cost of these cigarettes?"

"Oh. I show him my boobies."

"What?"

"Yeah, that's it, and he gives me them."

"No. That's wrong. You're a child."

"It's not like I'm whoring myself out. Just a flash here and there."

"That's how it starts. But this man is a predator. He will lull you into a false sense of security, and then he will pounce, and you might not survive."

Kylen looked down at me and saw that I was struggling to keep from fainting, "Dot? Dot? What's wrong?"

My mind was racing as I fought to keep conscious. "Look out behind you," I said as I saw a figure looming out of the darkness with an ether mask that he shoved under her chin. He picked her up suddenly, forcing the air from her lungs, and she inhaled the vapors. Then I blacked out.

The Kissing Spot

I was reminded of when I snuck off to the 'Kissing Spot' to meet with Harold Blackwelder. It was on a dare. They said that he liked me and wanted to kiss me. He was always a quiet boy in school but always seemed a little off to me. There was nothing that I could put my finger on; it was just a weird feeling. The stupid things that eighth graders do for fun in the middle of nowhere. I got there with my two witnesses, and so did he. So, we both completed the dare. Now, to go through with it. We sat down on a log, and the spot overlooked the town. It was right off a logging trail and as good a place as any. I didn't rightly know what to do, and I don't think he did either. He leaned forward, and so did I, but I held back. He stopped, opened his eyes, and said, "What?"

"I dunno."

"Well, come on. We're both here," he said, leaning forward again.

But I put my hand on his chest and said, "Wait a second. What did you have for dinner?"

"Spaghetti, why?'

"Your breath smells like garlic, and it stinks."

"So now what? he said as he turned away, miffed, and folded his arms in indignation.

"Hang on. I've got a solution.", I said as I reached into my purse for the last stick of gum and tore it in half. I'm handing him his piece. He looked down and nodded in agreement. We both unwrapped the gum and put it in our mouths. We started chewing and stopped and tried again after a minute or two. We crashed into each other, and everyone could hear teeth clacking. So, we mutually pulled back and caught our breath. Then we tried again, this time even slower. But we just bumped gums, and that hurt. There were tears in both of our eyes. I didn't think that we were ever going to get this correct. Well, he just lost it and slapped me hard. "You little tease. Get it right!"

Well, I had had enough. I was shocked and couldn't believe what was happening. I was so mad that he was blaming me for our youthful inexperience. So, I closed the distance and gave him the lesson that old Wilford had taught me. I remember him saying, "Dot if a boy ever gets fresh with you. You make him SING. Punch him in his solar plexus, stomp on his instep, smash his nose, and pop him in the groin. Make him SING.!"

And I did. I did all of the above for Harold in front of everyone. He never was the same around me after that day.

This snapped me out of the fit, and I could see that the assailant had Kylen down on the ground and was opening her nightgown. I reached behind me and found the toiletry bag. I couldn't stand and was still in the wheelchair. I rolled it forward swiftly and whirled the bag like a flail, screaming my fool head off, "YOU CAN'T HAVE HER!" He spun around and shot his foot out to stop the chair, but the momentum carried me forward, and the bag slammed into his head, and gravity kicked in and sent us both sprawling. I crashed into the hard tile floor and rolled to the right, swinging the bag again. I heard a bone crunch and a man cry out in shock. He flew into me and slammed my head back into a wall. I saw stars and fought to keep awake. His free arm was wrapped around my throat, trying to squeeze my life out. It's a good thing that I shattered his arm. Otherwise, I might have ended up dead. The toiletry bag was hanging between us, and he said in a rough voice, "Just die already, you bitch! I can still use you while you're warm."

As my brain was starving for oxygen, I remembered the rest of that evening at the 'Kissing Spot.' When Wilford arrived, the rest of the kids ran off. He saw that Harold had slapped me and what I did to him. He just motioned for me to get into the car. "I saw what you did back there."

"Yeah, I used SING on him. Just like you showed me.", I said, full of false bravado.

We drove silently for a few minutes, and I felt Wilford was measuring his words.

"Great. But sometimes, SING is just not enough. That's only good for boys who get fresh with you. I taught it to you to keep you safe. They taught us a Goshun-Jutsu self-defense technique in the army before sending us off to France. They even taught it to the nurses. Since it can be used by anyone who doesn't have enough strength, but it's not enough if you are face to face with someone who means to do you great bodily harm.", he said as he parked the car. I got out and saw we were in the back of the station.

"What are we doing here?" I asked nervously.

"There is something that I want to show you."

We went inside, and he took us through the white double doors and strode with a purpose over to body drawer #6. He opened it. It was about chest-high for me. "Dot, this here is Carolyn. Carolyn, this here is Dot."

I looked down and could see bruises on her neck. He continued, "Now Dot, Carolyn was out after dark and attacked. Note that this girl is college-age and fully grown. But her assailant, who strangled her, was a man, and he was bigger and stronger than her. He wrapped his hands around her throat and choked the life out of her. Understand this. The man will almost always win in a fight between a man and a woman because you cannot match his strength. So, it would be best if you used your wits and cunning. Please find a way to hurt him. Make it so expensive that he doesn't want to deal with you. Bite, scratch, claw. Put your fingernail into his eye until it pops. Slam both of your hands into his ears. Tear off his, well, you know. Use your wits. Fight dirty! You have to survive! SCREAM AS LOUD AS YOU CAN! Make a ruckus. Get people to stop what they are doing and come to your aid. Grab a rock and throw it at an oncoming car. Get away from the shadows and into the middle of the street. Run away as fast as you can and get to a well-lit area. Make him BLEED!"

I was fighting against blacking out, and I reached into my toiletry bag, and my hand found the comb. It was a woman's comb that came to a point at the end. I don't know why they issued it to me and kept the forks as a restricted item. I wrenched that comb out of the bag, flipped it around using it like a shiv, and stabbed him several times in the chest. I both heard and felt a lung deflate. He screamed, and it sounded like a gutted lamb. He shoved me away from him and ran out of the room. I heard shouts and voices coming down the hall. There were flashlights and what sounded like Jack Boots coming down the hallway. I tried to cry for help but could only manage a weak croak. So, I reached down, grabbed the ether canister, and launched it with what remained of my strength at the frosted windowpane, which shattered. They all turned as one and rushed into the room. I was sliding down the wall and doubling over, close to passing out yet again.

"Here they are." a voice yelled as a flashlight scanned the room.

Smelling salts were pushed under my nose, and I came too. “RAPE!” I cried. “RAPE!”

A soft, elderly, German-accented, cultured male voice said, “We hear you, child. You’ve been assaulted. Not raped.”

“No! He was trying to rape Kylen.”

“Who?”

“Kylen. The girl that has been showing me around the hospital.”

“I’m sorry. I don’t know which patient you are referring to. “

“Number 18.”

“What is your number?”

“23.”

My vision cleared, and Charlton reached down, gingerly picked me off the ground, and placed me in the wheelchair. “Sir, she needs to get to medical real bad. She’s got a concussion and..”

“Where did you receive your medical training?”

“France, Summer of 1917.”

“I see then. You are familiar with bodily attacks and the trauma that goes with them. Fine. Take the little troublemaker away.”

As he wheeled me down the hall, he whispered, “Dot. I don’t know what you got yourself into, but this isn't good. Very bad for you. I saw the blood on the comb and the trail leading away. So, I know that you got a piece of him, and if I find him, I’m going to crush the life out of that cat.”

“Hopefully, he’ll just crawl into a hole and die.”

“Why would you say that?”

“Because I punctured his left lung.”, I said rather smugly.

"Oh dear."

"What?"

"They don't like it when something like this happens."

"Yeah, me neither. I'm not a fan of assault, battery, attempted rape, attempted murder, and necrophilia."

"Necrophilia?"

"Yeah. The bastard said I was just as good to him, still warm."

"Stop it."

"Why? It's the truth."

"I know, girl, but the sound makes my blood run cold, and I want to vomit."

"How did you think it made me feel when he said it?"

"It made you want to fight for your life!"

"Which I did. By the way, he has a broken arm, so he didn't kill me. He couldn't. But not for lack of trying."

We stopped at the table where I had my spinal tap, and he gingerly picked me up and placed me on the examination table. A nurse came in and said to him. "You need to leave."

He went to turn away, but I didn't let go. "No! He stays."

She seemed to think better of it and pulled the privacy screen around. "Now let go and put your arm through there. Now, we can start the examination."

He was nervous, but I could see his anger when Kaylen and I were assaulted and almost raped while he was only a few feet away. The nurse cleaned my head wound and then moved on to the more critical exam part. She looked down below and said into a Dictaphone. 'Patient does not show any trauma to the perineum.

Hymen appears to be intact. She has several defensive wounds as she fought off her attacker. There appears to be blood that is not related to the patient.' How did you injure him?

"With a comb."

"A comb?"

"Yes, the pointy end that you use to tease your hair. I used it like a shiv and deflated his left lung."

I could see Charlton hang his head at that remark.

She continued. 'Patient is concussed, exhibiting signs of trauma to the skull. She needs to be observed for 24 hours And not allowed to fall asleep.'

"Okay. Button up.", she said to me. She lightly tapped his hand, and he let go. She swung the privacy screen out of the way, and he picked me up and placed me back in the wheelchair. I could tell that he was disappointed. "Dot, I tried to warn you."

"About what?"

"About these people here."

"What about them?'

"These people are hammers."

"Hammers?"

"Yes, and what do hammers do?"

"They collide with anything that sticks out."

"And to a hammer, everything looks like a nail. If anything sticks out, they want to beat it back into place. They don't care that you are an outpatient for tuberculosis and meningitis treatment. They don't care that you were assaulted and almost raped. They don't care that you were fighting for your and Kylen's lives from a monster.

They only care that you injured another human being with a comb and don't show remorse. Now they are going to start thinking that you are the addled one. That's a bad spot to be in. If you have any friends or family, contact them post haste because you will need it. Write as many letters as possible, and I will get them out for you. Tell your people what happened, as you will be scheduled for a sanity hearing."

My blood ran cold at the absurdity of it all. But then again, why not? I mean, I had damaged the calm of the facility. Never mind that they employed a monster. A sick, twisted individual who preyed on minors and the helpless. There was a special place in hell for this kind of being, and if I ever got the chance, I would gladly send him there. But I couldn't say it. Think it; sure. But not let them have the satisfaction.

I would have to tread lightly. The following 24 hours would be quite a task because, as tired as I was, I couldn't fall asleep. This would get weird as I had fought off two epileptic seizures in one day, and I don't think my brain could handle any more trauma. But I sucked it up, got a deck of cards, and played solitaire, Slap Jack, and War. Then, I switched over to Gin Rummy and Finally Bridge.

The morning came, and I was off for a spinal tap and breakfast. When I got my fried egg on top of a bowl of rice, I took the chub of milk and asked if they could heat it for me, which they obliged, returning it in a white mug about ¾ full. I then added the rice and some sugar and had rice pudding.

I got an orderly to take me down to the gym for exercise. They sat me in a chair and told me to try to lift my feet up and back again ten times. I was sweating by the tenth try. I was only out of commission for a month, but my feet felt like lead. This was perplexing. And the three times weekly spinal tap didn't seem to be helping my motor functions. I did notice that my arms were more muscular now since

I had been using them to get around. But I wanted to walk. Nay, run, which I couldn't do trapped in this chair.

I never did see Kylen again. Her bed was empty, and everyone acted like she didn't exist and had never existed. She was my only friend here. This absolute house of horrors. But now that I had seen the wizard behind the curtain, I felt they wouldn't let me leave. So, I wrote those letters, and Charlton snuck them out for me.

The Sanity Hearing

True to form, the sanity hearing was held roughly three weeks later. It turns out that there is a courtroom in the asylum. It makes more sense to bring the handful of people they require to settle the cases rather than transporting everyone there. Not a bad use of the taxpayer's money, and it keeps everyone safe.

I was brought before a panel and asked to explain myself. The panel consisted of several members of the board of directors and a judge. Two nurses escorted me in, made me sit at a table, and swear on the good book. That Dutch doctor Van Meeter with the cultured accent started right up.

"Can you tell us what transpired the night of the 25th?"

"No sir, I cannot."

"Cannot or won't?"

"Cannot, sir, because I was in a coma for a month, and no one bothered to tell me the date. They let me know what day it was but not the date. So, no."

"Can you tell us what transpired before you were discovered by myself, two orderlies, and a cook?"

"Well, let's see. Kylen and I.."

"Who is Kylen?"

" You would know her as Patient 18."

“Are you sure about that?”

“Yes, I am.”

“Well, I know we do not have a patient corresponding to that number.”

“Is that so?”

“Quite right.”

“Ok, bring him in.”, I said.

The Bailiff turns around and goes down the aisle to open the door, and Charlton stands. He is brought in and made to stand in the witness box and swear on the bible. Then Doctor Van Meeter started asking questions. “So, Mr. Charlton.”

“It’s Mr. Wiggins. Charlton is my first name.”

Fine, then, Mr. Wiggins. What can you tell me about this fictitious patient 18?”

“Well, her name was Kylen, and she is not fictitious. She was here for several months as a tuberculosis patient. She liked to come by the kitchen and play with the cats.”

“Why would you have cats in a kitchen?”

“We don’t. The cats stay outside and keep the rodents at bay.”

“So, how can you prove to us that such a patient exists?”

“Well, that’s easy. When an outpatient is sent here, they are given two pieces of metal, like dog tags, with their Patient Number on them. One goes on a string around their neck, and the other goes on their toiletry kit. Their names are engraved on the back.”

“Very nice story, but what does that have to do with anything here?”

“If I may?” he asked the judge as he undid the bracelet he was wearing, which was a copper band about 3x3 and tied with string.

The Judge looked at it and said to the stenographer. " Let the record show that the bracelet Mr. Wiggins provided me with has the number 18 engraved on the front and the name Kylen Murphy on the back."

"That doesn't prove anything."

"Well, Dr. Van Meeter, you can make records disappear and even move patients around, but you can't always get rid of everything."

"I believe you have made your point. Let's continue. Can he be excused?"

"Yes, but he must stay for the whole of the proceedings as his insight might be invaluable.", said the Judge.

"Ms. Dorothy-Jane."

"Yes?"

"Why did you attack another person?"

"I didn't attack anyone?"

"Yes, you did, and you are lying!"

"I defended myself and my friend Kylen from a rapist who used an ether mask to knock her unconscious." "And what were you doing while this was happening?"

"I was having an epileptic seizure."

"So, you were not conscious at the time?"

"I blacked out right as he was knocking her out."

"And, then what?"

"Then I woke up and saw him looming over her unconscious form, unbuttoning her nightgown."

"What did you do?"

"I rolled my wheelchair forward and swung my toiletry bag at him."

"So, you attacked him."

"NO! I defended her."

"By attacking him."

"Doctor, I don't understand your line of questioning."

"Neither do I," said the Judge. "Keep it on point."

"The point is she meant to harm another individual greatly."

"The point is she is describing beating off a RAPIST!" reminded the judge. "Someone that you claim never to have hired. So then, what is an individual doing on your property if that is the case? Miss, you may proceed without interruption."

"Thank you, Judge. Like I said, I swung the toiletry bag at him and hit him in the head. He shot his foot out and stopped the chair, so the momentum tossed me forward and onto the ground. I hit hard, swung the toiletry bag again, and broke his arm."

Doctor Van Meeter raised his hand, "Your honor, if I may?"

"Tread lightly."

"Understood."

"Miss Dorothy-Jane, what did you have in that toiletry bag?"

"One bar of soap, one toothbrush, a tin cup, a towel, two feminine napkins, two washcloths, and two combs."

"My, my. No bricks?"

"No. Why?"

"Because what you are describing, breaking his arm is impossible with the bag's inventory."

"Doctor, are you aware of the size of the bar of soap that they issue to us? It's supposed to last a month, so it is the size of a brick."

The judge asked the bailiff to "Produce exhibit "A."

He did, and it was a female toiletry bag. He dumped the contents onto the table and hefted the soap bar. Then, I placed them all back in and swirled them around. Then slammed it down onto the table, and it made a dent.

"Getting back to the point at hand. You fought this man off of your friend and wounded him. Then why were you the aggressor?"

"What?"

"You stabbed him several times."

"I'm sorry, but you don't seem to grasp that he slammed my head against the wall and used his free hand to try and throttle me. Bring out Exhibit 'B.'"

An envelope was opened, and the panel saw the scene of the attack. How many stitches, the defensive wounds, and the bruises on her throat. They were horrified.

"Your honor, I must protest in this vainglorious attempt at grandstanding…"

"That's enough, you. Allow the panel to review the record."

After they had looked through the pictures and tossed them away, shuddering, she knew she had made her point.

The judge asked the panel, "Shall we resume?"

They nodded assent.

"Can at least one of you say you are ready to proceed?"

A weak chorus of "Aye." came forth.

"So back to you stabbing him."

“I used what I had on hand to disable my attacker.”

“Why?”

“Because of what he said.”

“And what was that?”

“Okay, begging the courts to pardon the language will get rough.”

“Proceed.”

“He said in a rough voice, ‘Just die already, you bitch! I can still use you while you’re warm.’

“Seriously?”

“Yes, Doctor Van Meeter. So, I only had one choice: to use anything I had to stay alive.”

“So, you used a comb to stab him?”

“Yes.”

“ So, you admit to stabbing him when you wouldn’t say it before.”

“Because you kept acting like I was the danger. I defended myself. There is a difference.”

“You used violence.”

“The alternative was death and necrophilia. I’m not a fan of either. Not to mention the assault, battery, and attempted murder. Oh, am I making you uncomfortable?”

“Let’s move on.”

“No! Let’s not. I have made my actions crystal clear and find these proceedings abhorrent. You, Doctor, are making me out to be the danger instead of finding out who did this. “ Your honor, are we done?”

"Yes, I believe that we have heard enough. Now, would the panel like to retire to deliberate?"

The foreman stood up and said, "No, your honor, we have our decision."

"Is it in a written form?"

"Yes, sir."

"Then please read it."

"We find the accused to be of sound mind. She acted in what any sane, rational person would do in a time of extreme danger. We do not find her demeanor contrary nor her actions without merit."

"So, say you all?"

"A Chorus of 'AYE'" thundered across the room.

"Thank you for your service. You may retire."

The members of the panel stood up and left the courtroom.

Not to be outdone, the good Doctor had one more trump card to play.

"Your honor, in the interest of safety, I think it would be best that Ms. Dorothy-Jane be placed in an internal quarantine setting."

"What do you propose?"

"We have an isolation ward where the patients can be segregated…"

"Is it in Gen Pop?"

"I'm sorry, what?"

"Is what you propose to be in the General Population of the Asylum?'

"Naturally."

Denied."

"She must stay in the Tuberculosis Wing of the hospital. Period. No exceptions."

"We don't have a Tuberculosis Wing. "

"She must stay with the other Tuberculosis patients and doctor. I am beginning to lose patience with you."

"Miss Dorothy-Jane. You have been deemed of sound mind by the panel. Therefore, you will leave these premises as soon as your treatment course ends."

"Do you have anything to add?"

"I have a question for Doctor Van Meter."

The Judge nodded and said, "Ask away?"

"Doctor Van Meter, I was conscious for two days in the TB Wing of the hospital and only ever saw nurses. You didn't even turn up until after I was attacked, but you didn't do any Doctoring; you acted like a plant manager.

"Is there a question in there?"

"Yes. What is the doctor-to-patient ratio?"

"We like to think more of a staff-to-patient ratio."

"I wasn't asking that."

"Answer the question.", said the Judge.

"300 to 1. Though I hardly think that matters."

"It does. That's it. I'm done. Thank you, your honor."

In the end, there were too many questions and not enough answers. I was sent back to the hospital and placed in isolation. Well, that was fine with me as the medicine they had been giving me in the spine finally started to kick in, and after every spinal tap, I just wanted to sleep. The next thing I knew, it was three months later. I was bored out of my mind.

I started writing letters thanking everyone who helped me along the way. I was remiss in thanking Jordan for driving me to the hospital. As I contemplated what to write, I began considering my interactions with him in the past year. He started hanging out at the diner a lot, and I remember always seeing him reading a book in his hand. People thought he was sweet on me, and I disabused them of that notion. He was just a nice guy that had an overprotective daddy. He almost always got the same thing. A bowl of soup or chili and either iced tea or coffee. Biscuits or cornbread, whatever he was in the mood for. I asked him about the reading because it was pretty esoteric. It's not your standard fare. He replied, “I just want to broaden my horizons.”

“I think you want to broaden someone else’s horizons,” I said playfully.

“I don’t know what you mean..” he started.

“Oh, come on now. All the girls know that you are absolutely moon-eyed over the head librarian.”

.And why not? She was an attractive woman in her mid-thirties.

He blushed and said, “Dot. Don’t make a scene.”

“I won’t. I admire you. You have taste. And she’s a lovely lady and could show you a thing or two.”

“Is it wrong?”

“Is what wrong?”

“For someone as young as me to want her?”

“Nope.”

“But what would people say?”

"Who cares?"

"My daddy and the whole town."

"Well, Jordan. Maybe it's time for you to man up."

"What does that even mean.?

"Weren't you paying attention in history class?"

"You lost me.", he said, frustrated.

"Damn the torpedoes, full speed ahead. Just ask her out. You've already turned 18, and we are graduating soon. Take a leap of faith."

"But what if she laughs at me?"

"She won't. I see the way she eyes you as well. Be a man and ask her out."

"But where to?"

"I dunno. The movies over in Troy?"

"But what if we are seen?"

"Then you are seen. Treat her with respect. Don't flinch. Be there for her. Librarians need love, too."

And so, he finally worked up enough courage to go up and ask a woman who was 15 years his senior out. And lo and behold, she said yes!

Then, I also remembered the night that they got caught together. It was late May, and they had been seeing each other for a bit, furtively sneaking off, and then I guess either they got lazy or just too randy. They had parked behind the diner, and some bushes were installed for privacy, and they utilized them. Well, Jordan's daddy was looking for him and caught them making out. I was dumping trash when I heard the commotion and yelled, "Shelby, bring the bat and the shotgun. We got trouble out back!"

He complied and was there in an instant. “What’s the row about?”

“I dunno, but I heard some shouting and a slap.”

We both heard a woman sobbing. I ran over to her and saw it was Mrs. Sherry, the librarian. She had a palm print on her face, and her blouse was torn. Jordan was staring down his daddy and had taken quite a few licks. “Don’t you ever touch her AGAIN!” he yelled.

“But son, she’s no good for you. She’s a widow and damaged goods.”

Jordan snarled,” Back off, old man, or I will kill you!” he said as his daddy closed the distance.

“She’s old enough to be your mother!”

That was too much, and Jordan charged his daddy and knocked him out cold.

I got her on her feet and went back to the diner. We put her in the back, covered her with a blanket, and got her some warm soup. The sheriff was called, and Mr. Belfry was arrested for accosting Mrs. Sherry. He really couldn’t understand why he was in trouble and protested mightily.

“I can’t believe that you are arresting me for this.”, he said, motioning to the fact that he was handcuffed.

“Well, you can’t lay hands on a woman in my county and get away with it.”

“But I was just trying to protect my boy from this. This... hussy.”

“You shut your mouth, Mr. Belfry. You are the one in the wrong.”, I said.

Old Wilford said, “You just can’t get out of your way, can you Dot?”

“I ought to slap him on principle.”

“I’d like to see you try.”, Mr. Belfry said.

I marched over and slapped him good, even though he was handcuffed.

“Undo these things, and let’s do this proper.”, he said to Wilford.

“You ain’t gonna run, are you?”

“No. Wilford. But I don’t think it's right to have been slapped while I can’t defend myself. Besides, where would I go? This here is my home.”

“You won’t be able to.”, Wilford said in a measured voice.

“Young lady. Get back over her, and let’s do that again. Correctly, this time.”

Mrs. Sherry charged from behind me and threw a glass of soda directly in his face.

He nodded in approval. Then he wiped the soda off his face and said, “Girl, come here.”

Wilford nodded. So, I complied.

Mr. Belfry said, “I have the utmost respect for you. Because you were trying to right a wrong, but it wasn’t your place. I took that slap you gave on behalf of the woman I accosted, but it still was not your place. It was my son’s place, and he did do it. Now, here’s how this works. If a woman is ever accosted or insulted by a man, she has the right to deliver one slap in her defense. If he continues to insult or assault her, then she has a right to a second slap. If the man presses his luck, she can ask any man available to come to her aide. Now, she did you one better. She threw a drink in my face, which says that she won’t even sully her hand to touch me. The only other thing she could have done that was even a lower insult would be to spit upon me, but she is too much of a lady to do so. Now, it is my turn to apologize. Madam, I have wronged you. I didn't do it out of cruelty; I just wanted what was best for my son. But he fought for you, which means you are worthy of him. Okay, take me away."

So old Wilford marched him to the car and took him to the county jail.

After all this wool-gathering, I began writing my letter to Jordan.

Dear Jordan,

Thanks very much for driving me to the hospital in Troy. I'm sorry I haven't been able to write you before now. I was in a coma, and the medicine they gave me had me in and out of consciousness.

How are things between you and Mrs. Sherry?

How's your daddy taking it?

Take care

Dot

About ten days later, I got a response.

Hey, there Dot,

Thanks for thinking of us. Things are grand between her and me. We drove over to Troy and got married at the courthouse about mid-June. We didn't want a lot of fanfare. Just take it easy and do things kind of quietly. We went down to Mobile for a honeymoon and spent a week. We saw the sights and took photos with a brownie camera. Mobile is a busy place, with everyone rushing around. We even went to this place called an automat. Did you know that they are open 24 hours a day? Seven days a week. Something like this could put you out of a job. I also found out that Sherry snores like a wounded lioness. I swear I hardly got any sleep the first whole week that we shared a bed. She also told me that I snored loudly as well. So, it's always a race to see who can fall asleep fastest.

They have a lot of neat things to see and do here. We went to a vaudeville show in this grand old theater called 'The Sanger'. According to the guidebook, it took over a year to construct in 1927 and cost a whopping $500,000, but you can see where they spent all the money as it has three-color auditorium lighting, a large organ, and full stage facilities. The front entrance is grand, with ornamental Greek Statues of Poseidon and Dionysus. Not to mention that the curtains are made of crushed red velvet and the seats match and are very comfortable.

My daddy begrudgingly came around and ordered us a little bungalow from the Sears catalog and had workmen assemble it. He gave her the house and 40 acres as a wedding present and told her they were hers, no matter how things worked. She's a few months pregnant, and the baby is due in March. Hopefully, you will be able to come home before then. She looks absolutely radiant, and I want to spend every waking hour with her. But unfortunately, I can't since we have the ranch to run.

Thanks for everything

Your pal,

Jordan

Well, now that was a pretty nice turnout. It could have gone so differently. As I had too much time on my hands, I decided to keep busy. So, I requested books from the library and started reading as many as possible. I read books on law and procedure. Contracts and Agent Theory. The texts were pretty dry, so I requested the recordings of the actual classes; they were in two formats, reel to reel and 78" records. There were even question-and-answer sessions incorporated into the lectures. Call them if you still have questions; a message service will take the request. Then, either your questions would be incorporated into the class, or they would send a postcard with the responses.

I took a business correspondence course for actual college credit and completed it. Working the sums took a while, as math was never my strong suit. But I worked at it, and it was work. It probably took me twice as long as everyone else to complete the course, but I did and was given a certificate of completion. I didn't know if it would get me anywhere in life, but it couldn't hurt my job at the diner. And who knows, maybe I could bring some new ideas to Shelby at the diner.

Finally, there was the day of my release from the hospital. I turned in my hospital gown, slippers, and blue robe. They let me keep the toiletry bag and its contents, with blood stains and all, plus the two panties they had issued me. Inside the toiletry kit, I had about two dozen recipes that I wanted to try out as soon as we got back home. Since my clothing had been cut from my body and burned in an abundance of caution, I was given a rack of clothing I could choose from that had been donated by local churches in the area. I picked out two outfits. One set of dungarees with a checkered top with cape sleeves and a scarf, with red tennis shoes. Then, a gunny sack dress with a lovely flower print, a belt, some sensible brown shoes, and socks to match. I took no bra since I had no breasts to speak of. One of the nurses took pity on me and came around and picked up a box full of lace and flowers. She handed it to me and said, "Darling, take this, please. You will grow into it over time, and every woman needs a nice piece of underclothes."

"That's mighty nice of you. But I don't think I can ever fill out a bra. I'm built like a 15-year-old boy, and here I am, 18 and all."

"She pressed it into my hands anyway and said, "Time will tell."

I thanked her and walked out into the sunshine and the waiting arms of old Wilford and Doc Stevens.

“Not to put too fine a point on it, but Dot, you look like you’ve been to the wars.”

“Well, in a way, I have. I hope I killed that sumbitch.”

Wilford spoke up, “Dot. I’m sorry we failed you.”

“Y’all didn’t fail me. Y’all did everything within your power to keep me alive. The state is the one that failed me. I’m just glad to be rid of that place. I’ve just lost six months of my life and feel like I’ve just been paroled from prison. So, can we stop at the nearest diner and get a bite to eat? Because I’m starving.”

“Sure, we can.” Old Wilford said joyfully, “Dot, what are you having?’

“Steak and eggs, with grits, biscuits, and gravy. Then, a whole thermos of coffee. Those Mormons in there don’t have coffee or tea. “

“I think I’ll just have some pancakes and hot tea.”, said Doc Stevens

“Well, I’m going to have Salmon and Croquettes with chicken gravy and black coffee.”

“Sounds divine.”, I said as we drove off to the nearest diner.

The diner was located about two miles away from the hospital. It was an old dining car from a train, and the food they served was wonderful.

“So, Dot, what’s the first thing you will do when you get home?”

“You mean besides giving Delbert a five-minute hug and messing up Anthony’s hair? I mean to take a long warm bath. Then, I’ll set to work trying out some new recipes.”

“Like what?’, asked Doc Stevens.

“Pigeon and mushroom stew.”

“Sounds nice, “said Wilford.

I’m thinking to myself, maybe it’s time to go after the insurance company on behalf of how they futzed up Daddy’s insurance policy.

PREVIEW Of

"A Time to Shine"

Book 1 in the Patrol Craft Series

USS ABERDEEN: Morning Watch Underway Heading to the Coral Sea

Daniel Core stared at the coffee cup dregs and felt the turbines speed up. He was dressed in a Navy work uniform, a soft collar chambray shirt with bell-bottom dungaree material pants, a navy blue knit belt, and a cover also dyed Navy blue to protect it from heavy soiling generally only worn by the gunnery and engine room departments. He focused on the Vmail that his mother had sent him. A new way of corresponding with soldiers, seamen, and airmen stationed abroad used a standardized stationery template incorporating the letter and envelope together. They were filled out, copied to film, sent to the destination, enlarged, and printed. This reduced the cost and space for mail; thousands of letters could be combined into a few rolls of film.

VM To: Daniel Core	From Penelope Core
Destroyer USS Aberdeen	1315 Ashley Phosphate Rd.
Pacific Fleet, Pearl Harbor	Charleston, SC

December 17, 1941

Dearest Son,

I have not heard from you and worry you need to eat more. We learned of Pearl Harbor's devastation and hope you are well. There is so much talk about an invasion, and rumors are flying. Your brothers have joined the Marines and Army, respectively. Midora has also decided to serve and has joined the WAVES. So many of my children have joined the war effort, and I can say nothing. I know that you are doing what you must to protect us all. I am proud of you all.

With much love,

Mother

'There's that wicked shimmy again,' he thought as he felt the ship's deck plates shift. "They need to get that handled." He pocketed the letter, grabbed his metal tray, and placed it and the heavy porcelain coffee cup missing a handle in their respective places. He headed for the turret at frame 5, Gun 1.

It was an older ship commissioned in the 1930s when the treaties declared she could only be so many tons. But she was built with two oiler stacks instead of the typical four. She used updated steam injection technologies to increase turbine rotation plus a 22% increase from the earlier classes. There were only eight officers and a full battle complement of 250 other ranks, 50 Marines. They were performing escort duties to and from Australia.

He remembered last week when they had been moored alongside the USS Minneapolis during the attack at Pearl Harbor, dispatched several aircraft, and helped sink a mini-submarine in the bay. Then, they charged forward to set up a screen to protect the bay against a third wave that never came.

"That was a hell of a day," he thought as he made the usual twists and turns to get to his duty station across the 377-foot-long and forty-foot-wide ship.

He had joined the Navy in 1939 when he witnessed German U-boats sinking ships from a convoy launched from Charleston, SC, headed to Britain. He even had a Captain's ticket as his grandfather had been a tugboat captain and wanted to leave the business to a family member, and he had been the only one interested. So, he had worked tirelessly to earn that Captain's Certificate, and then the world went crazy. After witnessing the destruction of the ships, he went home, and when he walked in, his grandfather just knew. He didn't have to say anything. He just got up and began packing a seabag, handing it to him.

"If a good man does nothing, then that is evil enough. Go forth and help conquer that evil. But remember, you will only be a wheel in a cog. They will tell you your place. Please don't fight with them or argue because cream rises, no matter what. Your time will come." They got in the truck and headed to the induction site. He disembarked, never looking back. The Navy sent him to primary, then on to gunnery school. He made it to the rate of second class and was rather good at what he did but always struggled with math. He had an eidetic memory, so he could call up tables if he had read them at least once, which significantly helped him in life. The Navy was not interested in his Captain's ticket because he had yet to go to college, nor did he even know any of the right people, so being an officer was right out. They wouldn't even consider him for a Warrant Officer, which he felt was a little unfair, but then he remembered his grandfather's wisdom and just shrugged it off.

"Hey, Core?" called a voice from behind a cabinet.

"Yeah, Cortez?"

"Here's your fiver from last night's game," a smallish Mexican American from Los Angeles said as he slapped the currency into his hand. He was dark and swarthy compared to Daniel's ghost-white complexion. His black hair - not quite curly or straight - wouldn't commit, but the Navy haircut took care of that.

"How did you know?" Cortez asked.

"Know what?" asked Daniel.

"That they were going to win?" said Cortez.

"It just seemed like it was their time. After all, the cream rises!"

"Ejo de puta.," Cortez said half-jokingly. (*You son of a bitch.)*

"Yo, intiendes tu dece," (*I understood what you said*) Daniel said with a half-smile as he sat at the desk and pulled out the file on the ammunition expenditures. Switching to English, he said, "We've been firing our guns almost too much lately, and if we don't watch it, the bores will crack, and it will be back to the yards to replace them."

"So what? Then we leave this 'Mierda' and get a few weeks of Liberty in San Diego. We can get some good tamales and Chorizo plus Horchata, which we could use in this heat."

"You got that right. Horchata would be nice. But sometimes it's too much, too sweet and filling. I prefer just a plain coconut cooled under ice, top sliced off with a straw in it," he said as he undid his top button and pointed the desk fan towards himself.

The overhead Klaxon went off. "GENERAL QUARTERS! GENERAL QUARTERS! Aircraft spotted! All hands to Battle Stations!"

They both jumped up and scrambled to reach Turret 1, right outside their office, donning helmets and life vests. They jumped inside and battened down the hatch. They climbed into their seats, donning communications gear. As soon as the hatch was dogged, the light switched to the red bulb, indicating battle mode. Their job was to coordinate the ship's fire control to the target. They had an Officer above them, but he oversaw four-127 mm guns. His name was Mr. Begley, and his voice came over the comm. "Turret 1- target bearing 472-Azmuth 151.3. Mark!"

"Turret 1-target 151.3 Aye!" they called out in unison.

"What say you?" he asked.

Looking through the scope, Daniel saw the outline of what appeared to be a minesweeper or oiler from the Japanese Navy. “Sokaitai!” he called.

"FIRE!" came the order.

"FIRING!" he yelled as his foot stomped on the mechanism, and a 127mm shell was launched toward the enemy. Clicking and whirring noises sounded as the ammunition elevator raised a shell and a powder bag, and two crewmen lifted them out and placed them into the firing chute.

He could hear the Antiaircraft guns firing outside. But he had to focus on the task at hand. "Firing, firing," he called out as he mashed the pedal twice. Then, they waited.

"Miss! Close! Hit! Keep firing. We got the range right!"

So, they did. They kept it up until the command, "Turret One-Cease Firing! She's done for." He heard and felt the explosion across the water slam into his turret.

"Turret One-here. How close were we, sir?"

"They crossed the T!" Mr. Begley called out, meaning they had lined up perfectly for destruction.

He was glad but sad as they had just killed or doomed 200-300 people, but he reminded himself that was the price of war. "If they hadn't attacked us, we wouldn't be in this mess!" A dark look crossed his face as they stowed the gear and returned to the office. Mr. Begley was already there, looking incredibly pleased with himself. He was a good officer who kept track of his men: a typical tall, lean blond from a Navy family, Annapolis graduate, Captain of the Football team, and wearing the khaki uniform of the day. As he whipped out his notebook, Cortez reflexively jumped to the typewriter and loaded it with paper.

As soon as it was charged, Mr. Begley said, "Morning watch after-action report. 07:38 General Quarters sounded. Aircraft spotted approaching DU-Greg 151. Turrets 1 through 4 responded to sightings of several Maru to the lee. They were targeted and destroyed as they Crossed the T. 31 rounds were expended, and 5 minutes elapsed until contact was broken. AA gun emplacements under command downed five enemy fighters. Approximately 450 rounds were expended. No torpedoes were launched as an approach not attainable. Convoy suffered no losses. "

"Send it!" he stated, holding his hand for the copy and leaving the compartment to deliver it to the Captain. Daniel retrieved his copy, running down the corridor to the radio shack that would encrypt it and send it back to Pearl.

Midwatch

Daniel and Cortez were just in the middle of the mess hall when Mr. Begley walked up to them, motioning for them to follow him. They complied, and he took them to the front of the chow line and signaled the cook. He came forward with two trays full of steak and potatoes. They both looked at the perfectly prepared steaks, and their mouths watered.

Mr. Begley whistled loudly and said, "Now hear this! Turret 1 sank a minesweeper this morning, and they are rewarded with steak. Do your job right, and you will eat well, too. That is all." He motioned for them to sit at an unoccupied table. The crew members looked on as they ate chipped beef on wheat toast. Also known as SOS – 'Shit on a Shingle.' But no one was jealous. They were glad for their brethren. But they also knew the steaks would be tough. So, they smiled and nodded at the good fortune, knowing their turn would come.

Two others joined them at the table- Chris McConnell, a tall, skinny man from Pennsylvania who was of Armenian stock, and Steve McCaskill, a ghost white man of 5'4" with curly black hair and just a dusting of freckles across his face- who were the loaders for the 5-inch guns. Chris smiled at the steak. Daniel nodded, cut it in half, and forked it over. Chris nodded at Cortez, who leaned over his plate and said, "No way, man. It's been too long." He looked longingly at the steak.

"That's not quite fair. They loaded the shells that we fired," said Daniel

"Too bad! Plus, I had my wisdom teeth removed last time we won steaks, so it's even!" replied Cortez.

Chris nodded, then cut his steak in half and gave it to Steve.

"Queen to Bishop six, check," said Daniel.

"Knight takes Queen," replied Chris.

Steve had pulled out a small travel chessboard and used a book to hide it. They had to rely on their memories for this game. Steve looked over the board, recording the moves and checking for accuracy.

"Bishop to King 7, check," said Daniel.

Most of the lunch-goers were now crowding around and beginning to place bets.

"Bishop to King 7, checkmate!" called Daniel triumphantly.

Chris needed clarification. He said to Steve," Verify!"

"Verified!" replied Steve dejectedly.

Chris reached over to shake Daniels's hand when an explosion rocked the ship—lifting it and slamming it down. Red emergency lights popped on, and they scrambled to their feet as the secondaries went off. The boat rocked and leaned hard to starboard. Screaming could be heard over the con. "Get replacements to the bridge; Daniel Core, report to the bridge!"

He rushed forth past the confusion and tried to block out the destruction. When he arrived, the bridge was no more. It had been peeled back, and the wind was whipping about; a shocked helmsman named Restivo was frozen in place. "What are your orders?" He called out.

Mr. Begley was lying in the Captain's Battle Cabin bed with blood pouring from his chest. His face was wan and tight. He motioned for Daniel to come forth. "We got hammered! All the officers are dead. I'm promoting you to Warrant with acting Captaincy. Choose the replacements from what is left of the crew and fight the ship!" His voice rasped, and blood filled his mouth.

"Sir?"

"The Captain himself wrote the orders. You were our backup plan. Here's the battlefield commission. He wrote it when you struck for Warrant. Don't mess it up," he said as he pressed a manila envelope into Daniel's hands. He reached up and pinned the rank to his collar.

"Helm, I stand relieved," he called out as he died.

"Helm, what's our heading?" Daniel asked crisply, trying to stay focused.

"192," he yelled back.

Daniel reached over to the com and hit the switch. "Now hear this! Damage reports to the bridge by runner. All officers are dead. I, Daniel Core, am now in charge and acting Captain. I need all trained reserve personnel to the bridge. Repair parties and fire control teams report to your stations. All Marines split into parties of 10 and help in any way possible." He closed the switch.

"Helm, what hit us?"

"Two torpedoes and a big bomb." The helmsman winced as a corpsman applied a large bandage to his cheek.

Daniel could hear the replacement crew members pulling bodies out of the way and dragging them down the corridor. Buckets of sand were tossed liberally around. They could wash the blood and entrails later. Right now, they just needed to survive.

The next few minutes flew by as he ascertained the damage to the ship and attempted to keep pace with the convoy and keep the lookouts busy, watching for everything. He knew that they had to reduce speed to help fight the fire. If he went too fast, it would just fan the flames. "Helm reduce speed by 50 percent."

"Reducing speed by 50 percent, aye."

"Helm, What's our speed now?"

"Uhm, 20 knots, sir."

"Good! Keep her there."

He heard the sound of a freight train crashing directly in their path and saw the lead cruiser take a hit from a shell that exploded into a gun mount. The cruiser was rent open, white steam escaping from jagged holes as he saw her list to one side.

He called the order out, "Helm hard starboard. Avoid hitting that cruiser and screen her from further attack!"

"Hard to starboard, Aye!" the helmsman called out expertly.

"JESUS CHRIST! Collision, COLLISION! Ship to Port" called a watcher.

"HELM HARD, LEEWARD!" Daniel screamed as a destroyer loomed from the white fog spilling out of the cruiser. They barely missed each other as collision alarms and bells rang out.

Suddenly, they heard a "WHUMP" sound as a small support ship slammed into something and exploded. The radio said, "CONVOY, CONVOY; you're in a minefield! All craft head east now! EXECUTE!" He saw a PBY buzz by and was grateful for the assistance. Those Amphibious planes resembled albatrosses and were their eyes in the deep.

He gave the order, and the ship veered wildly to the side, and he heard her groan. He also saw HMS 136 and HMS 119 laying down a smokescreen to help protect the cruiser. DD134 drifted through the fog, and he heard a rattle and whump, then saw the ship lift and slam down again. He called to the lookout, "What just happened to 134?"

"They rolled a depth charge overboard, and it exploded too close underneath her and took out her propellers."

"All 5-inch guns fire to protect 134!" he called out.

"Why aren't they finishing us off?" he called to no one. Then he walked over to the port side and saw roiling smoke from multiple rends in the ship. He realized this was now the fog of war, and they couldn't hit what they couldn't see.

"Helm, come to 162, head for the atoll anchorage. "

"Maru sighted on the starboard side," called a replacement crewman. The Maru, a converted Merchant ship, sported guns and torpedoes.

"Marines report to rear starboard side armed to repel all boarding parties," he called out. The order was relayed through the PA system.

"All antiaircraft guns open up on that, Maru! Fire for effect!" he said. He heard a different type of boom starting to ring out from the ship's rear. "Waisner, what's that booming?" he asked.

"It's the Marines, sir. They are using anti-tank weapons," Waisner, a beefy Scotsman from Salkehatchie, SC, replied.

"Well, that's creative," he said.

www.ingramcontent.com/pod-product-compliance
Lightning Source LLC
LaVergne TN
LVHW010703110826
845149LV00014B/3210

* 9 7 8 1 9 5 8 2 9 7 5 8 2 *